On the Road with Mark Twain in California and Nevada

George J. Williams III

Tree By The River Publishing
P.O. Box 935-O
Dayton, Nevada 89403
To order books call Toll Free 1-800-487-6610

On the Road with Mark Twain in California and Nevada
by George J. Williams III

Published by:
Tree By The River Publishing
P.O. Box 935-O
Dayton, Nevada 89403

To order autographed, inscribed books with *Visa* or MasterCard, call **1-800-487-6610**, 9AM-5PM, West Coast time seven days a week.

Other non-fiction books by George Williams III:

Mark Twain: His Life In Virginia City, Nevada (1986)
Mark Twain: His Adventures at Aurora and Mono Lake (1987)
Mark Twain: Jackass Hill and the Jumping Frog (1988)
Rosa May: The Search For A Mining Camp Legend (1980)
The Guide to Bodie and Eastern Sierra Historic Sites (1981)
The Redlight Ladies of Virginia City, Nevada (1984)
The Murders at Convict Lake (1984)
The Songwriter's Demo Manual and Success Guide (1984) revised 2nd edition 1994
Hot Springs of the Eastern Sierra (1988) revised 2nd edtion 1993
In the Last of the Wild West (1992) revised 1994

Library of Congress Cataloging-in-Publication Data
Williams, George, III, 1949-
        On the road with Mark Twain in California and Nevada/ by George J. Williams III
        p.   cm.
        Includes bibliographical references and index.
        ISBN 0-935174-20-6: $27.95.—ISBN 0-935174-25-7 (pbk.) : $12.95
1. Twain, Mark, 1835-1910—Homes and haunts—California.
2. Twain, Mark, 1835-1910—Homes and haunts—Nevada. 3. Authors.
American—19th century—Biography. 4. California—Description and travel.
5. Nevada—Description and travel. 6. California—Biography.
7. Nevada—Biography. I. Title
PS1334.W56 1993
818'.409—dc20
[B]   93-31
                                                                             CIP

Written, published and printed in the United States by American craftsmen.

CONTENTS

Those who honor me, I will honor...
1 Samuel 2:30

I think that much of my conduct on the Pacific Coast was not of a character to recommend me to the respectful regard of a high eastern civilization, but it was not considered blameworthy there, perhaps...I think all my references can say I never did anything mean, false or criminal. They can say that the same doors that were open to me seven years ago are open to me yet; that all the friends I made in seven years, are still my friends; that wherever I have been I can go again--& enter in the light of day & hold my head up; that I never deceived or defrauded anybody, & don't owe a cent. And they can say that I attended to my business with due diligence, & made my own living, & never asked anybody to help me do it, either. All the rest they can say about me will be bad. *I can tell the whole story myself, without mincing it, & will if they refuse...*
Mark Twain to his future father-in-law Jervis Langdon, December 29, 1868

Ah, well, I am a great and sublime fool. But then I am God's fool, and all His works must be contemplated with respect.
Mark Twain in a letter to William Dean Howells, 1878

Why I wrote this book and Why you should give me Your money

When I studied literature in college a millennium ago, Mark Twain was the writer who made me laugh. It wasn't a silent laugh or a muffled snicker. It was a yuk-yuk laugh that came from my tummy and made me feel good. Twain made me feel good. I know my experience reading Twain wasn't unique. The world laughs when it reads Twain.

Like every English major, I was required to read some of the dullest stuff, man ever put to paper. Today when I come across those miserable writers whose dreary work I was forced to read to earn my degree, I wish I could resurrect them so I could roast them at the stake.

Ah, but Mark Twain. Spending time with him was like spending time with a pal—like when you were a kid and got the sillies before bedtime, when every word out of your mouth was hysterical and you laughed till your stomach hurt.

Ah, for the weary English major, reading Twain was a pleasure. Here was a human being with a brain in his head, a heart in his chest and brave enough, smart enough, to write like human beings spoke. And write about things we can relate to. Reading Twain, I didn't have to wade through endless paragraphs crammed with useless words, bad writers use to impress other bad writers. Reading Twain was fun.

So I cared for Twain as I did not care for other writers. I admired his ability to laugh at himself. Twain knew the human race because he had gotten to know himself. He was aware he could be a fool as each of us are capable. Understanding his strengths and weaknesses caused Mark Twain to have ambivalent feelings for the human race; he could be amazingly compassionate and fiercely condemning.

Equally impressive was Twain's ability to articulate his understanding simply. Twain could say in one sentence what other writers could not say in a book. Like this:

> Be good and you will be lonesome.
> *Following the Equator*

Anyone who has tried with all his heart to behave himself knows how impossible and lonesome it can be. In a single sentence Twain turned a serious insight into a humorous phrase we can understand.

So, back in college Mark Twain's writings were the bright spots in a drab career as a student. It probably doesn't mean squat to you. But it's my book, so I thought I'd tell you.

One day while reading *Roughing It*, Mark Twain's second deliberate book in which he tells about his experiences in the Far West, I was made aware how important his years in Nevada and California were to his career. They provided him with a reservoir of experiences he would pour into his books over his lifetime. Most importantly, Twain's Western years gave him the Jumping Frog story which launched his international career.

But I never learned that in college. In fact, I can't recall a single professor telling us about Twain's Western years and their importance to his career. It was always the Mississippi River and Sam Clemens as a steamboat pilot and Negroes and slavery and "Swing Low, Sweet Chariot," and all that Southern stuff. Not a breath about his life in the Far West where Clemens first wrote under "Mark

Twain" as a struggling Nevada reporter. I don't know, maybe those Ivory Towered know-it-alls who spin their wheels somewhere between here and the real world aren't impressed with Twain's Western years.

I am.

For instance, *The Innocents Abroad*, Mark Twain's first book and a great success when published, was largely based on correspondent letters Twain wrote for the San Francisco *Alta California*. Although Twain began the book in Washington, D.C., he completed the manuscript in San Francisco. This, as other important aspects, was never pointed out by any professor in any Twain class I took.

There have been writers who have written books and articles about Twain's Western years. Some have done good jobs and I respect and thank them for their labors. However, since the publication of these works new Mark Twain letters have been discovered. Besides, it is the nature of literary and historical research, the more one digs, the more one finds. Which means it is time to update the information available about Twain's Western years.

My personal difficulties with some of the former works are: some writers do not explain why Twain's Western years were important to his later success; they casually talk about places in the West as if Eastern readers are familiar with them. The books are often without current maps to the historical sites where Twain lived and wrote. Their books often lack the rich collection of historical photographs of the places Twain lived and the people he knew. Nor are there current, accurate road directions to historic sites. You sometimes get the impression that some writers did not physically retrace Twain's Western years on the ground. In other words, some writers seem to have not done their footwork. (Of course, my being the perfect writer and scholar, I have done the best job possible within my imperfect humanity.)

My purpose in writing the *Mark Twain in the West* series, is to one, familiarize readers with Twain's years in California and Nevada which were crucial to his writing career; two, to introduce readers to the California and Nevada mining towns where Twain lived; three, to introduce to readers the men who influenced and helped Mark Twain's early career; and four, to collect rare photographs of the places where Twain lived and the people he knew.

Having done this, I believe readers and scholars will discover that if Sam Clemens had not lived in the Far West, his life, his writing and his eventual success would have been vastly different. In fact, it may have never happened.

In my *Mark Twain in the West* series I have dedicated each book to a particular period of Twain's Western career and covered that period intensely. *Mark Twain: His Adventures at Aurora and Mono Lake*, tells about Twain's arrival in Nevada and his first year as a prospector and miner. *Mark Twain: His Life in Virginia City, Nevada*, details Clemens metamorphosis from failed miner to hard working journalist. *Mark Twain: Jackass Hill and the Jumping Frog*, covers Twain's departure from Virginia City for San Francisco, his work as reporter and free-lance writer and his trip to Jackass Hill where Twain discovered the Jumping frog story which launched his career.

Differing from my previous books, *On the Road with Mark Twain in California and Nevada*, covers Twain's entire Western career. This book is a hands-on guide for Twain scholars and readers to Twain's haunts in California and Nevada. Maps and directions will lead you to the places where Twain lived and wrote. I tell you what Twain did at each place and provide lots of information about the towns and country. Great efforts have gone into locating and publishing the rich collection of photographs of historic sites, buildings and Twain's contemporaries.

In my efforts to unearth Mark Twain's life in the West, I have spent more than a half dozen years traveling across California and Nevada. It has been a pleasure. In the process I've written four books on Twain's life—one was selected for a Pulitzer Prize--and I've covered a grocery bill or two. And I plan to make a documentary film on Mark Twain's Western career.

My primary sources for the *Mark Twain in the West* series are: the letters Mark Twain wrote while living in the West; the letters and correspondence of friends and family who knew Mark Twain during these years; the newspaper and magazine articles Twain wrote during this period, and finally, articles written about Twain at the time and afterward.

Secondary sources are the writings of Mark Twain, primarily his notebooks kept during this period, and such Twain works as *Roughing It, Sketches New and Old,* and *The Autobiography of Mark Twain,* which at times are unreliable due to Twain's love of exaggeration and his sometimes faulty memory.

Whenever possible I have let Twain and others speak through their writings. Why not let the witnesses speak for themselves understanding not all they say or write is gospel? Overall, I believe this works for the reader and scholar. Having these witnesses speak for themselves gives us a reality that paraphrasing, inordinate commenting, and rationalizing do not. Important sources are either listed before or after long quotations or in brackets within paragraphs. I'm sorry, I think footnotes are distracting and bothersome; why not just name the sources and get it over with?

I have taken particular efforts with dates, telling what Mark Twain was doing on what date and where. I am not fond of dates. But I believe the Mark Twain fans and scholars will appreciate my efforts for it will save them a good deal of trouble. The Chronology in the Appendix alone is worth the price of this book.

In this book you and I will go bouncing down the back roads of California and Nevada into the mining camps, mountains and towns where Mark Twain lived the most adventurous years of his life and grew as a person and writer.

But we won't travel as Twain did, in stagecoaches, wagons, by horseback or on foot. No way. Not us. We're gonna do it in a blazing red convertible with the top down so the sun and wind can blow in, a stereo with blasting rock n' roll and two seriously built blondes in the back seat. It'll get us in the mood.

I'm lying.

In this book you'll learn some things about Mark Twain even those Ivory Towered know-it-alls don't know and it'll be fun and interesting besides.

So here we go. Let's have a good time.

Carson City, Nevada
Spring, 1994

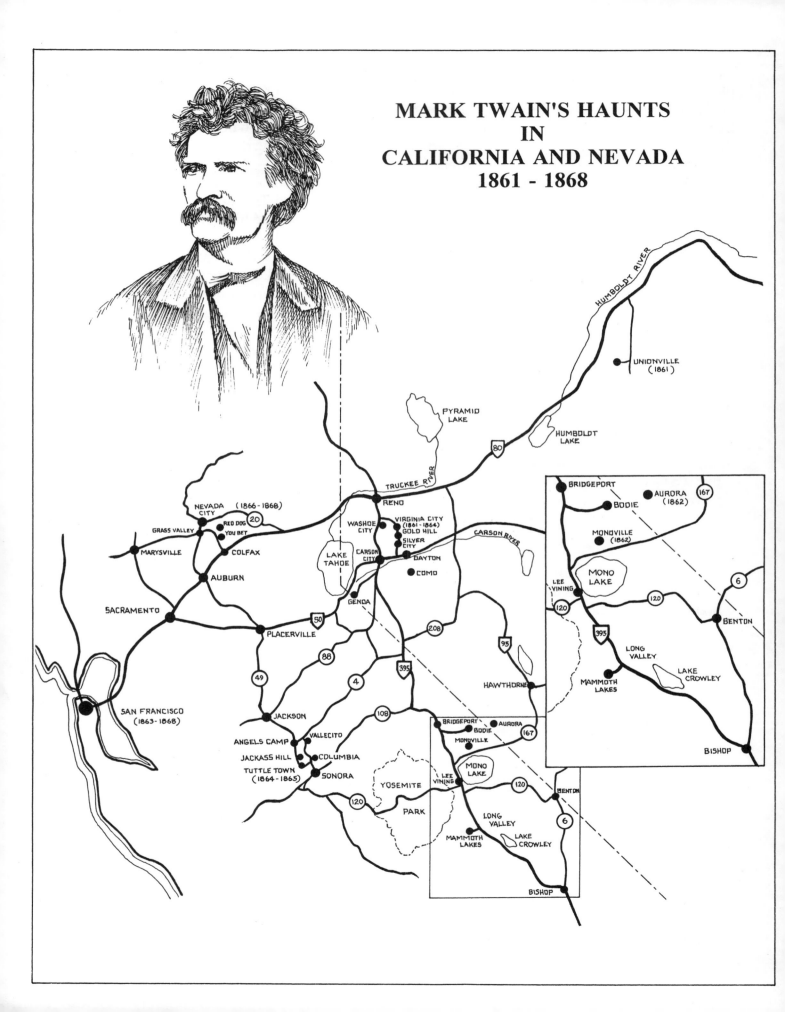

MARK TWAIN'S HAUNTS
IN
CALIFORNIA AND NEVADA
1861 - 1868

Part 1
Steamboat Pilot, To Timber Rancher, To Miner

Sam Clemens, "Mark Twain," as he looked when he worked for the *Territorial Enterprise* in Virginia City, Nevada 1862-64.

"Mark Twain" was not born in Missouri as most of us have been taught. Mark Twain, the writer, the character, was born amidst the bitter odors of whisky, gin and beer in John Piper's saloon in Virginia City, Nevada, when Virginia City was a rip-roaring, take-your-life-in-your-hands, rich silver mining town atop the Washoe Mountains south of today's Reno.

Piper's "Old Corner Saloon" was the hangout for Sam Clemens and other Virginia City reporters and printers who daily ground out the Comstock Lode's several newspapers. The Bohemian crowd gathered at the Corner Bar after they put their papers to bed or at "coffee breaks" during the day which were frequent and necessary. Clemens had the habit of going into the bar with at least one friend. He ordered drinks for himself and his pal and asked Piper to "mark twain," meaning, mark two drinks on the wall behind the bar. That's where John Piper kept track of his customers' tabs. Clemens' newspaper friends picked up on this behavior trait and began calling him "Mark Twain." Clemens began using the pseudonym shortly after in a dispatch from Carson City, January 31, 1863.

Clemens in later years wanted to bury his reckless, hard drinking years in the West. It was not good for his image as America's premier author and moral voice. To do so, he concocted several stories about the creation of his famous pseudonym; neither wash when examined today.

His favorite story was that he had stolen the name from a New Orleans writer who had

Orion Clemens, Sam's older brother and Secretary of Nevada Territory. Right, Orion's wife, Mary "Mollie" Clemens.

died; diligent research has never discovered this writer. Another was that "mark twain" had something to do with measuring the depth of the Mississippi River. Both stories were more or less accepted by the public and plausible. But I am convinced it is the Piper's bar story that is the truth. While Clemens lived in the West more than one friend figured he would "fill a drunkard's grave" if he did not change his ways. On at least one occasion he spent a night in a San Francisco jail for drunkenness. His reputation for drink was well known in Virginia City.

All right. So we know Clemens drank hard as a young man. But we also know that drink did not kill him nor did it substantially interfere with his life and work. Nor did Clemens become alcoholic. In later years Mark Twain succeeded in using the tamer stories to cover his tracks for his reckless years in Nevada and California.

Mark Twain spent nearly five and a half years in Nevada and California between August,
1861 and July, 1868. He arrived as a twenty-five year old unemployed steamboat pilot and left as a popular writer and celebrity. During this time he made a five month stint to the Hawaiian Islands (then the Sandwich Islands) in 1866 and a five and a half month cruise to Europe and the Holy Land in 1867. Clemens returned to San Francisco in March, 1868 after his voyage. He left California and the Far West for good July 6, 1868. His "Jumping Frog of Calaveras County" story, discovered during a stay at Angel's Camp, had already been published in newspapers throughout America and Europe; Mark Twain was well on his way to international literary success.

On a miserable scorching day of August 14, 1861, a curly headed stranger with a body like an elf and a head like a bowling ball, fell out of the stagecoach doors in front of Carson City's Ormsby House hotel. He was powdered with a layer of white dust from crossing the dusty Carson Plains. He looked like he had been rolled in flour and prepared for baking. He was tired, sore and sorry he had ever agreed to go along with his older brother Orion [Or-ee-un] to Nevada Territory. Clemens then believed the barren Nevada wastes had been created by

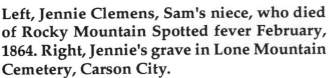

Left, Jennie Clemens, Sam's niece, who died of Rocky Mountain Spotted fever February, 1864. Right, Jennie's grave in Lone Mountain Cemetery, Carson City.

the Devil for his personal torture. All the two brothers had seen for days were sagebrush, white alkali wastes and barren ranges of mountains. By the time the Concord coach skid to a weary halt in front of the Ormsby House, Clemens was powerfully thirsty.

I'll bet Clemens found the nearest saloon—probably the one right in front of him, the Corner Bar at the Ormsby House, dragged his sorry self inside and had a whisky. I'll bet he had more than one. And I imagine that he and his brother stayed in that saloon all afternoon until Carson City's heat cooled. And then Clemens and his brother stepped outside into the early evening to discover the hell they had agreed to live in.

What brought the brothers to Nevada was Orion's misfortune of being named Secretary of Nevada Territory by Ed Bates, a member of Lincoln's cabinet and a friend. I guess this was Ole Ed's idea of a joke, sending poor Orion, the kindest but least prepared human being for

reality, to Nevada Territory. Little did the two brothers know what they had gotten themselves into. But in the end it would be all right. It would be more than all right for Sam. He would leave the West Coast seven years later as one of its most well known and popular writers headed for international celebrity. But arriving in Nevada, Clemens was not a professional writer but a steamboat pilot. But that's another story.

At the age of twelve following the death of his father in 1847, Sam Clemens asked his mother if he could quit school to become a printer's apprentice to help support his family. She agreed. Clemens learned to set type in a Hannibal, Missouri newspaper and print shop becoming familiar with every aspect of newspaper work and the publication process.

Clemens was a bright and precocious boy and continued educating himself as a voracious reader. By fifteen he had read the Bible and many of the works of Cervantes, Goldsmith and Hood. After he found a page from a book about Joan of Arc in the street, Clemens developed a serious interest in history. Clemens was highly curious, had a precocious understanding both of words and human nature

James Nye, Territorial Governor of Nevada. Twain lampooned Nye in *Roughing It*, as the leader of the Irish Brigade.

and he was a good speller.

He began writing, largely to amuse himself and by seventeen had managed to publish a story in an Eastern magazine. After completing his printer apprenticeship, Clemens worked as a printer and editor for two of Orion's village newspapers, one in Hannibal, Missouri, another in Keokuk, Iowa. Occasionally Clemens wrote humorous articles in which he poked fun at local characters.

At seventeen, Clemens began traveling throughout eastern America landing newspaper work as a printer and typesetter in St. Louis, New York City, Philadelphia and Cincinnati. During this time he wrote travel articles for several newspapers. In these early letters we can already see a young writer, keenly observant and able to articulate his observations and feelings with wit and satire.

In 1857, at the age of twenty-one, Clemens left newspaper work and spent the next four years on the Mississippi River as a steamboat appren-

tice/pilot. Had the Civil War not disrupted river traffic in the spring of 1861, Clemens may have stayed a pilot. But with the closure of free river traffic with the war, Clemens was suddenly out of a good paying job.

So in August of 1861, Clemens, twenty-five years old and with nothing better to do, tagged along with Orion to Nevada for the fun of it. He intended to stay in Nevada a few months and go back home. He stayed, off and on in the West, for the next seven years.

In Nevada he had hoped to earn a living as Orion's personal secretary. When he learned his pay would be deducted from Orion's meager salary, Clemens decided to try something else.

Sam visited nearby Lake Tahoe (then called Lake Bigler) in the Sierra mountains above Carson City. There on several trips in August and September, 1861, with Tom Nye and John Kinney, he laid claim to hundreds of acres of timber. Clemens filed legal papers which gave himself and his relatives claim to the timber. But timber was an unexciting business.

Clemens then turned his interest to silver and gold mining. Northwestern Nevada Territory at this time was in a frenzy of mining activity due to the huge strikes of gold and silver at Virginia City, 15 miles northeast of Carson City. The California Gold Rush of 1849 was long over. When gold and silver were discovered at Virginia City in 1859, thousands of young California miners crossed the Sierra in hopes of making their fortunes. Clemens along with the others became infected with the madness and roared off on wild goose chases to the mining camps of Aurora in September, Unionville in December, and back to Aurora from April to September, 1862. The trips were costly and unsuccessful.

Cooped up in his cabin at Aurora during the spring thaw of 1862, Clemens began writing humorous letters about the trials and tribulations of a hard-luck miner. He signed the letters "Josh" and mailed them to the *Territorial Enterprise* in Virginia City where they were pu-

The original Ormsby House where Sam and Orion landed in August, 1861.

liished. Editor Joe Goodman was impressed by the "Josh" letters and believed the writer wasworth cultivating. Goodman was at this time looking for someone to replace Dan De Quille in the autumn of 1862 as a local reporter. "Josh" seemed a likely replacement. Goodman offered Clemens the reporter position in July, 1862. The following September, somewhat reluctantly, broke and discouraged, Clemens left Aurora for Virginia City and his new job. [For more on Mark Twain at Aurora, read the author's, *Mark Twain: His Adventures at Aurora and Mono Lake.*]

Carson City, Nevada

Some people are malicious enough to think that if the devil were set at liberty and told to confine himself to Nevada Territory, that he would come here and loaf sadly around, awhile, and then get homesick and go back to hell again. But I hardly believe it, you know, Margaret wouldn't like the country, perhaps—nor the devil either, for that matter—or any other man—but I like it.

Sam Clemens, in a letter to his family February 8, 1862

Sam Clemens arrived in Carson City August 14, 1861 with his older brother Orion who had been appointed Secretary of Nevada Territory. Clemens, except for brief trips to Lake Tahoe and Aurora, lived in Carson City during the fall of 1861. He left for Unionville in December but returned by mid-January, 1862. Clemens stayed in Carson City until April when he left for a six month stay at Aurora, Nevada.

Mark Twain covered the Territorial Legislatures at Carson City as a reporter for the *Enterprise* in November and December, 1862 and November, 1863 through February, 1864. During this time Twain roomed in Carson with his brother Orion, wife Mollie, and daughter Jen-

The Corner Bar inside the Ormsby House Hotel where Clemens and other reporters gathered while covering the Territorial Legislatures. Twain's character Buck Fanshaw in *Roughing It*, in real life Tom Peasely, was gun downed here February 2, 1866.

nie at their house at 502 North Division Street at the northwest corner of Spear and Division. The house still stands.

Twain returned to Carson City in 1866 and 1868 and gave lectures at the Carson Theater.

Carson City is located in northwestern Nevada at the northern end of Eagle Valley at the eastern foot of the Sierra Nevada (that's Nuh-*veh*-duh not Nuh-*vah*-duh.) The town sits on what once was a sagebrush covered, sandy plain at 4400 feet. Carson City is 30 miles south of Reno and 10 miles east of Lake Tahoe. It can be reached from the north and the south by U.S. Highway 395; and from the east and west by U.S. Highway 50.

Carson City is the capitol of Nevada founded by Abraham Z. Curry who had emigrated from New York. Curry arrived in Eagle Valley in 1858. He and three partners bought all of Eagle Valley for $500 cash and a few horses. The three partners soon departed, two gave their shares to Curry, the other sold his share for a pony and 25 pounds of butter. The town was named after Kit Carson, the well known western guide and explorer who had passed through the area in 1844. Curry, a generous and community oriented man, believed Carson City would be the capitol of the state even before the area was known as Nevada Territory. In 1858 he wisely set aside four blocks of the central section as a plaza while the town was still being laid out. Today, the Capitol buildings occupy this site.

Carson City became a hot bed of activity in 1859 when gold and silver were discovered at Virginia City, 15 miles northeast. With the explosion of numerous silver and gold camps in northwestern Nevada, the infant town

Above, Carson City, Nevada in the 1870's.

boomed. Carson City became a center of economic and political activity. Timber from the nearby Sierra Nevada mountains provided lumber for the rapidly growing mining camps. Local businesses provided mining parties with everything from shovels and picks, to dried beef and beans. For nearly thirty years, Carson City was a beehive, full of prospectors and speculators, all hoping to get their hands on some of the gold and silver buried in Nevada's mountains. There were many hotels, lodging houses, saloons, restaurants and general stores.

From its beginnings, Carson City served as the political center for Nevada. Orion Clemens, elder brother of Sam Clemens, became Secretary of Nevada Territory in 1861. During the frequent absences of Governor James Nye, Orion served as Territorial Governor.

The Territorial Legislatures met in Carson City in the fall before the Territory became a state October 31, 1864. Abraham Curry offered his Warm Springs Hotel as a meeting place for the legislators. Curry even provided legislators with desks because the Territorial Government could not afford the expense. Today, Curry's old Warm Springs Hotel is the site of the Nevada State Penitentiary on east Fifth Street. Parts of the old hotel remain.

When gold and silver mining took a slump in the 1890's, Carson City's economy, along with the rest of Nevada, floundered. State government provided jobs and kept the town alive.

Today Carson City is a fast growing town of about 40,000 whose main business is state government. Along Carson Street there are several casinos. Lodging is plentiful on the strip and there are several fine restaurants, including Adele's on North Carson Street, decorated in the ostentatious Victorian style.

Like most American cities, Carson City has many franchises: typically, K-Mart, McDonald's, etc. RV parks and supplies are available in town along Carson Street.

Sights to see: The Capitol, State offices,

Governor's Mansion, Nevada State Library, Nevada State Museum, Nevada Railroad Museum, Nevada State Prison, Stewart Indian Museum and many fine Victorian mansions. You can find these historic buildings by picking up a tour guide map at the Nevada State Museum on Carson Street, or at the Visitor's Center on South Carson Street across from K-Mart.

Carson Hot Springs, on Hot Springs Road at the northern end of town, has a warm swimming pool, private spas and an RV campground.

Lake Tahoe

Three months of camp life on Lake Tahoe would restore an Egyptian mummy to his pristine vigor and give him an appetite like an alligator. I do not mean the oldest and driest mummies, of course, but the fresher ones.

Chapter 22 *Roughing It*

Mark Twain visited Lake Tahoe in late August, 1861, with a young friend, John Kinney. In September, he returned with Tom Nye and camped for three weeks on the eastern shore near Glenbrook and Zephyr Cove. He writes of his experiences in Chapters 22 and 23 of *Roughing It*. Twain returned to Glenbrook in the summer of 1863 for a short vacation.

Lake Tahoe is located in the Sierra Nevada mountains on the borders of California and Nevada, 10 miles west of Carson City. Lake Tahoe can be reached from the east by U.S. Highway 50; from the north through Truckee, California via California Highways 89 and 267 and from the west through Placerville, California on U.S. Highway 50. Two thirds of the lake are in California; one third is in Nevada. The gambling casinos are located in Nevada on the southern and northern shores.

"Tahoe" is the Washoe Indian word for "big water," "high water," or "water in a high place," all of which help to describe the great high mountain lake. Lake Tahoe is the second highest, large lake in the world. At 6,225 feet, it is 23 miles long, 13 miles wide with 195 square miles

Below, Orion Clemens' house Carson City. Photo was likely taken in the 1930's.

in surface area and a maximum depth of 1,645 feet.

It is believed that the first white men to see Lake Tahoe were the Captain John Charles Fremont party who reached the lake February 14, 1844. Fremont named it Lake Bonpland after a fellow explorer. In error, his map maker dubbed it "Mountain Lake." When Mark Twain first visited the lake in the summer of 1861, Lake Tahoe was known as Lake Bigler, named after a California governor John Bigler, who afterward was a notorious drunk in Nevada. In 1862, the name Lake Tahoe was adopted and has remained (probably due to Bigler's horrible reputation.)

Lake Tahoe is located in the deep Tahoe Basin. High forested mountains tower 3,000 feet above the lake. Water drains from the lake at the northern end through Truckee Canyon becoming the Truckee River which passes through Truckee and Reno. The Truckee River is Reno's main source of water.

Though primarily a tourist attraction today, in the 1860's, lumber mills around Lake Tahoe provided Carson City and Virginia City with enormous amounts of lumber and timber for shoring-up the Comstock mines.

Today there are numerous settlements around the lake: Rubicon, Meeks Bay, and Homewood on the western shore; Tahoe City, Carnelian Bay, Tahoe Vista, Kings Beach, Crystal Bay and Incline Village on the northern shore; Glenbrook, Cave Rock, Zephyr Cove, and Round Hill Village on the eastern shore and the City of South Lake Tahoe and Camp Richardson on the southern shore.

Sights to see: Beautiful Emerald Bay on the northwestern shore, Cave Rock on the eastern shore. River rafting is a popular pastime in the Truckee Canyon on the north shore. Ski lifts are available in winter (providing it snows); fishing, boating and water skiing are popular in summer.

Below, Abe Curry's Warm Springs Hotel, where the Territorial Legislatures met. Today this is part of the Nevada State Prison on East Fifth Street, Carson City.

The receipt for Sam and Orion's stage fare from St. Joseph to Carson City, Nevada.

Unionville

We were stark mad with excitement—drunk with happiness—smothered under mountains of prospective wealth—arrogantly compassionate toward the plodding millions who knew not our marvelous canyon—but our credit was not good at the grocer's

It was the strangest phase of life one can imagine. It was a beggar's revel. There was nothing doing in the district—no mining—no milling—no productive effort—no income—and not enough money in the entire camp to buy a corner lot in an Eastern village...

Chapter 29 *Roughing It*

Mark Twain, visited the silver mining town of Unionville with several men in December, 1861. He prospected there for about two weeks, became disgusted with the camp and returned to Carson City in early January, 1862. He writes about his experiences in Chapters 26-33 of *Roughing It*.

The Unionville historic site is 150 miles north-east of Carson City. To reach it, take I-80 at Reno and head northeast 125 miles to the Mill City exit. Then take Nevada Highway 400, 20 miles south to the Unionville site.

In August 1861 Indians arrived in Virginia City with tales of silver fortunes in the Humboldt Range. They brought with them silver ore samples from Buena Vista Canyon which assayed rich in silver.

Two men persuaded the Indians to guide them to the location. Ten days later the Humboldt Mining District was formed and the excitement of a new silver boom thundered through northern Nevada. "Humboldt! Humboldt," became the latest in a list of sensations. A town site was formed and named Dixie.Tensions brought on by the Civil War caused Unionists to rename the camp Unionville.

A lower town site was laid out in 1862. By the summer of 1863, there were about 1,000 people living in 200 cabins and houses. The camp had nine saloons, six hotels, four livery stables, drug stores, an assay office, a brewery, a newspaper, the *Humboldt Register*, whose main objective it seems, was to tout Unionville.

About three dozen mining companies were formed and scores of tunnels were drilled into the mountainsides. As is often the case, none of the mines paid off. Miners and speculators made money by selling and trading worthless mining stock. Unionville declined from 1864 to 1867. In 1868, a rich strike in the Arizona mine gave the town a brief second life. Three stamp mills were built and worked the Arizona's ores. In 1872 a fire destroyed the mill and investors lost interest in the town.

The last year of production was 1880 when 2.7 million dollars were produced in the district. Small operators worked the area into the twentieth century but there were little profits.

Stone ruins remain, a few old houses and a cemetery at the mouth of the canyon. There is a park at the head of the canyon for picnicking and camping. Water is available. You can camp in and around the area. Today Unionville has lots of apple trees and much wildlife. A wonderful spot for an autumn visit.

A hot spring is located on a dirt road about ten miles east and across the valley from Unionville; the water smells slightly sulfurous but it is plenty warm and clean enough for a good soak in the desert sun.

"Honey Lake" Smith's

By day we were all crowded into one small, stifling barroom, and so there was no escaping this person's music. Through all the profanity, whiskey-guzzling, "old sledge" and quarreling, his monotonous song meandered with never a variation in its tiresome sameness and it seemed to me, at last, that I would be content to die, in order to be rid of the torture. The other man was a stalwart ruffian called "Arkansas," who carried two revolvers in his belt and a bowie knife projecting from his boot, and who was always drunk and always suffering for a fight.

Chapter 31 *Roughing It*

Mark Twain was stranded at Honey Lake Smith's for about eight days in early January, 1862 on his return trip from Unionville. The winter rain storms had caused the Carson River to rise and made crossing it impossible. Twain stayed in the one room lodging house until the river calmed. He recounts his miserable stay in Chapter 31 of *Roughing It*. It is one of Twain's most humorous episodes.

Below, U.S. Senator William "Bill" Stewart's home in Carson City. Twain visited here.

The First Presbyterian Church in Carson City. Mark Twain gave his first paid-for lecture to raise funds to help complete the church. Orion, Molly and Jennie Clemens were members.

The old inn and trading post of "Honey Lake" Smith's is now under water at Lake Lahontan. The site is 2 1/4 miles east of Silver Springs, Nevada.

To reach the site from Carson City, take Highway 50, east 35 miles to Silver Springs, Nevada. Continue on Highway 50 east along the northern shore of Lake Lahontan. Near the western shore of Lake Lahontan, a dirt road heads south to the western shore of Lake Lahontan. The site of "Honey Lake" Smith's can no longer be seen or visited, unless you are a scuba diver.

Originally called Williams' Station, the name was changed when Honey Lake Smith took over the operation after 1860. Located on the Carson River along the highly traveled emigrant route to Carson City, Honey Lake Smith's provided lodging, food and some supplies to those passing by.

In April, 1860, after countless atrocities committed by whites against Indians, a Paiute band killed five men and burned Williams Station to the ground. This created a ruckus among the whites in Virginia City and Carson City. An army of about 105 men was organized by Major Ormsby, Nevada's version of General Custer. Ormbsy chased the Indians to Pyramid Lake where a great number of Paiutes were gathered and had prepared a trap for Ormsby and his men. The Paiutes, to Ormsby's astonishment, surprised his army and surrounded them. The ordeal was a major disaster for the whites when Ormsby and 60 soldiers were killed. The battle at Pyramid Lake was the culmination of a long list of wrongs done to the Paiutes by white men, including numerous senseless murders.

When Honey Lake Smith took over the operation, he rebuilt the cabin and added brick stables on a knoll above the river. It is my understanding that the brick walls still remain below the surface of the lake.

Lake Lahontan Dam stores water from the Carson River which is used for irrigation at nearby Fallon. The lake is a popular fishing, swimming and boating spot in spring and summer. Cottonwood trees along the shoreline provide excellent camping places.

Top, looking north along the eastern shore of Lake Tahoe where Clemens camped in August and September, 1861. Bottom, a rare shot of Unionville, Nevada, a silver mining town where Clemens tried prospecting in December, 1861. The trip proved costly and disappointing.

Left to right, A.J. Simmons, Samuel Clemens and William "Billy" Claggett. All three made their way to Unionville in December 1861 in search of mountains of gold. Disappointed, Clemens returned to Carson City in January, 1862.

Top, the barren and rugged mountains above
Unionville, looking toward Star Peak. Below,
ruins at Unionville near the mouth of the canyon.

Top, a grave in the Unionville cemetery at the mouth of the canyon. Bottom, the grave of Docia Lucas Bailey, killed by Indians seven months after Sam Clemens' trip to Unionville. Troubles with Indians, generally caused by whites, were still a problem in the out-back of Nevada.

Aurora

Esmeralda [Aurora] was in many respects another Humboldt, but in a little more forward state. The claims we had been paying assessments on were entirely worthless, and we threw them away. The principal one cropped out of the top of a knoll that was fourteen feet high and the inspired Board of Directors were running a tunnel under that knoll to strike the ledge. The tunnel would have to be seventy feet long, and would then strike the ledge at the same depth that a shaft twelve feet deep would have reached!

Chapter 35 *Roughing It*

Sam Clemens lived in Aurora from April to September, 1862 trying to strike it rich as a prospector and speculator. Twain writes of this time in chapters 35-41 of *Roughing It*. Clemens mining adventures failed. He left Aurora broke in September, 1862 for a reporting job on the *Territorial Enterprise* in Virginia City. There Clemens adopted his now famous pen name, Mark Twain.

What was supposedly his frame cabin at Aurora, was moved to Reno in the 1920's. There, through neglect and vandalism, it was eventually destroyed.

Aurora, Nevada, is located 130 miles southeast of Carson City and 23 miles southwest of Hawthorne, Nevada, the nearest town. The site is fairly accessible during spring, summer and fall by highways and graded dirt roads.

From Carson City, the quickest and easiest route is by taking U.S. Highway 395, 92 miles south to the Bodie State Park turnoff, 7 miles south of Bridgeport, California. Here take the Bodie Road 13 miles to Bodie State Park. Ten miles of the Bodie Road is paved, three miles are a well graded dirt road. Bodie is on your way to Aurora, and the truth is, there is more to see at Bodie than at Aurora. Interestingly enough, Clemens may have passed through Bodie on his way to Monoville in the summer of 1862.

Bodie was a booming gold mining camp 1878-82, though gold was discovered there as early as 1859; a few miners settled there in the spring of 1860. Today the old gold mining town is a ghost town and a California State Park. A visit to Bodie will give you an idea what Aurora was like. There is a small admission fee per car.

After visiting Bodie, to reach the Aurora site, go north around the Park and proceed 13 miles down Bodie Canyon. This road can be rough, even impassable, if the spring runoff has wrecked portions. It is wise to check with the Bodie Park rangers before heading down Bodie Canyon. I suggest you use 4X4 trucks.

Thirteen miles from Bodie, you will come to a sandy flats and an intersection. Turn right, and go four miles to the Aurora site. The Aurora Cemetery is a about a half mile this side of Aurora. A sign should point the way to the cemetery if someone hasn't stolen it or blown it away with a gun—which is not uncommon in these parts.

If you are approaching from Los Angeles or the Mammoth Lakes area, take Highway 395 north past Lee Vining about 8 miles to California Highway 167. This is also called Pole Line Road. Turn right, go east on Highway 167, 45 miles. About 5 miles this side of Hawthorne, you'll come to a well graded dirt road on your left, or north side. This road goes up and over Lucky Boy Pass and into a valley; it is known as the Lucky Boy Grade (the mining camp of Lucky Boy was located at the top of the grade.) Near Nine Mile Ranch, a road leads to Aurora about six miles away. Nine Mile Ranch is a large stone building. You can't miss it. If you pass the Ranch, you've gone too far. Back track.

By the way, there are no stores or gas stations at Bodie or near Aurora. Carry plenty of food, water and gas. If you breakdown out here, well, there you are. Unless some kind soul happens along, you'll by making like a jackass and hoofing it out.

Gold was discovered in Aurora in August, 1860 by three men who had struck out from the nearby mining camp of Monoville in the hills north of Mono Lake. Within two months

Aurora, Nevada about 1884. Clemens lived and mined here April to September, 1862.

propectors had made 357 claims.

In April, 1861 the first stage arrived from Carson City at Aurora. When Sam Clemens arrived a year later, Aurora consisted of about 2,000 frenzied miners living in everything from holes in the hillsides to crude stone shelters, tents and cabins. Many brick buildings were being built and there was the usual array of whorehouses, saloons, tent restaurants and stores.

By April, 1863 stages were bringing in 25-30 newcomers a day. The town had a population of 4,000; 200 were women and children. There were 761 houses, 64 of them brick; 22 saloons, 2 churches and 2 newspapers. The population eventually peeked at 6-10,000.

For a time it was believed Aurora was located in California. However, in October, 1863, a survey party determined Aurora was four miles within Nevada Territory.

By 1865, the initial excitement cooled. Surface bonanzas had produced 24 million dollars but much of the money was wasted by incompetent mining companies. By the end of the year, half the town had moved on to other camps.

When Bodie boomed in 1878, Aurora recieved renewed interest. The major mines were reworked but four years later the county seat was moved to Hawthorne, Nevada.

The Aurora mines were reworked in the early 1900's following the discovery of the cyanide gold extracting process. This ingenius process helped leach gold from mine tailings previously considered worthless. When World War I broke out, mining activity ended at Aurora.

Currently, a mining company is doing some open pit mining at Aurora.

Nothing is left at the town site of Aurora but a few foundations and rubble. After World War II, Aurora's abandoned brick buildings were dismantled and the brick was sold. It was a terrible mistake and a great historic place in Nevada was destroyed.

Top, Clemens' cabin at Aurora before it was moved to Reno where it was destroyed. Bottom, the graveyard at Aurora, Nevada today is in still fairly good shape.

Top left, Cal Higbie, one of Clemens' mining partners at Aurora to whom Twain dedicated *Roughing It*. Top right, John Nye's Nine Mile Ranch near the Walker River not far from Aurora where Clemens allegedly went to nurse Nye through an illness. Bottom left, Bob Howland, another of Clemens' mining partners. Bottom right, Howland at far left stands outside his stone cabin at Aurora with fellow miners. Both Howland photographs are very rare.

Clemens' June 22, 1862 letter to his brother Orion in which he describes where their "Annipolitan" claim was located in relation to the "Wide West" claim. The Wide West mine was rich in gold. Clemens for a time believed their Annipolitan claim may have been "mixed" with the "Pride of Utah" and "Dines" claims. If so, he and Orion would have a promising claim. However, not long after, Clemens discovered their claim was separate and therefore worthless. Clemens used this as the basis for the story of the Wide West mine in *Roughing It*.

This is a photograph of Clemens' mining deed dated March 1, 1862 on file at the Mono County courthouse at Bridgeport, California. This document shows that Clemens had bought interest in several Aurora mining claims. The following month, April, 1862 Clemens moved to Aurora.

Top, the road Clemens walked down as he left Aurora. Bottom, Bodie in 1906.

Bodie

Mark Twain is believed to have passed through the mining camp of Bodie in August, 1862 on a walking trip with Cal Higbie to Monoville, a small mining town just north of Mono Lake. Both men had been prospecting and mining at Aurora, Nevada, a silver mining town 17 miles northeast of Bodie.

Gold was discovered at Bodie, California in the autumn of 1859 by four miners, Bill Bodey, Pat Garraty, Terrence Brodigan and Bill Boyle. The miners had left their home base at Monoville and headed northeast into the Bodie Hills, prospected near what was to become Aurora, and then headed southwest up Bodie Canyon to the high mountain valley where they discovered gold at the base of Bodie Bluff. It becomes very cold in this valley at 8200 feet in the autumn. The four miners were unequipped to spend the fall and winter at their discovery site, and returned to Monoville. They promised each other to keep their gold discovery secret.

But back in Monoville, Bill Bodey broke his promise. He and "Black" Taylor soon returned to the site and began working their claim. They built a small cabin and prepared to stay at the site through winter. They made trips to Monoville for supplies. On the return of one of these trips to Monoville in November, 1859, Bodey and Taylor were hit by a surprise blizzard. The two men struggled through the snow but a mile from their cabin, Bill Bodey collapsed in the snow. Taylor tried to carry Bodey, but the man was too heavy for Taylor. Taylor decided to leave Bodey, return to their cabin, refresh himself and come back for Bodey.

By the time Taylor returned, the snow was deep and Taylor was unable to locate Bodey. In the spring they found what was left of Bodey. His bones had been stripped by hungry coyotes. Afterward there was a persistent rumor among the local miners that Taylor had actually murdered Bodey for the gold. Ironically, Taylor was murdered by Indians not long after at nearby Benton.

For the next seventeen years small numbers of miners worked the placer and hard rock gold deposits at the site. But not until a rich gold strike was made in 1876, did the town finally boom. For the next six years the town steadly grew and eventually reached a peak population of around 10,000. The gold camp became known as Bodie after Bill Bodey. A printer had misspelled Bodey's name to "Bodie" (pronounced Bo-dee) and no one bothered to correct the error. Bodie became widely known as the most wicked and lawless town in the West. Gunfights and murders were common.

By 1882, manipulation of stock prices by San Francisco stock brokers had caused havoc and distrust. The bottom fell out of the market and Bodie began its long decline.

The discovery of the cyanide gold extracting process at the turn of the century gave Bodie a new life. Mining continued until the outbreak of World War I. Mining resumed after the war into the 1950's, but the town dwindled year by year, and mining profits were slim pickings.

The State of California made Bodie a California State Park in 1962. The Parks Service looks after the old wooden and brick buildings which are kept in a state of "arrested decay." About a quarter million people visit Bodie each year. The town has become one of the most popular places to visit in the California Eastern Sierra region.

You may reach Bodie from the north or south by taking U.S. Highway 395 to Bridgeport, California. Seven miles south of Bridgeport a road leads thirteen miles into the Bodie Hills to Bodie. Ten miles of the road is paved; the last three miles is dirt road. RV's, campers and trucks with travel trailers can easily make it into Bodie. Please keep in mind there are no stores or gas stations at Bodie. Camping is permitted outside Bodie on Bureau of Land Management land. There is no charge. There are public toilets and a fresh water spring at Bodie. [Editor's note: For more information on Bodie and neighboring Eastern Sierra mining towns, read *The Guide to Bodie and Eastern Sierra Historic Sites*, by the author. See Appendix.]

Mono Lake

There are only two seasons in the region round about Mono Lake—and these are the breaking up of one winter and the beginning of the next.

Chapter 38 *Roughing It*

Sam Clemens visited Mono Lake in August, 1862. He and Cal Higbie rowed a boat out to Paoha Island and explored the volcanic island. On their way back to shore, Mono Lake became a raging sea and their boat nearly capsized. Mark Twain was one of the first to write about Mono Lake in Chapters 38 and 39 of his second book, *Roughing It.*

Mono Lake is located in the high desert Mono Basin near the center of California, just east of Yosemite National Park and about 300 miles north of Los Angeles. Mono Lake (pronounced *Mow*-no not *Mah*-no) can be reached from the north and south by Highway 395; from the east from Hawthorne, Nevada by Highway 167 (Pole Line Road) and from the east and west by Highway 120. Highway 120, which runs through Yosemite National Park, is closed in winter.

Mono Lake at 6,373 feet above sea level is sort of oval shaped being 13 miles long and 8 miles wide. It is the largest lake entirely in California. The lake is entirely surrounded by mountains and hills. To the west is the towering Sierra Nevada whose streams flow into Mono Lake. To the north are the volcanic Bodie Hills. To the south is an open plain, and rising above, the Mono Craters, huge, gray volcanic domes. Farther south again is the Sierra. To the east there is a long plain of sand dunes and sagebrush which rise in the far distance to pine nut covered, volcanic mountains.

The mountains and hills surrounding Mono Lake capture its waters; no water flows out of Mono Lake. Mountain streams and spring water entering the lake carry minerals and salts which are deposited and remain in the lake. These mineral and salt deposits have caused Mono Lake's waters to become three times more salty than sea water and the water is becoming more salty by the year.

Yet in what first appears to be an inhospitable environment for any form of life there is an extraordinary life system.

During the summer months, huge amounts of algae burst forth in the lake. The algae becomes food for millions of tiny brine shrimp which thrive in the saline waters. The brine shrimp population explodes in the warmer summer waters creating a massive food source for great flocks of migratory birds—California Gulls, Snowy Plovers, Wilson's Phalaropes, Northern Phalaropes, Eared Grebes and other birds which make Mono Lake their breeding and nesting territories during the spring and summer. The birds mate and lay their eggs on Mono Lake's two volcanic islands, Paoha and Negit, where the chicks hatch and are nurtured.

However, this extraordinary ecosystem was recently disturbed by man. In the 1940's, the City of Los Angeles acquired water rights to Rush and Lee Vining Creeks, the major sources of water for Mono Lake. The City diverted these streams into an aqueduct depriving the lake of 80% of its water source. This caused the lake to drop 45 vertical feet and caused a land bridge to form between the northern shore and Negit Island, where thousands of California Gulls and other birds nest each spring and summer. The land bridge enabled mainland predators to reach the Island; thousands of chicks were killed and a major nesting place was destroyed.

A suit initiated by the Audobon Society and the Mono Lake Committee at Lee Vining, has temporarily prevented Los Angeles from diverting Rush Creek into its aqueduct. The level of the lake has since risen and the land bridge to Negit Island has been covered, restoring Negit Island as a nesting place. Happily, the nesting birds have returned to the island.

Sights to see: Tufa Reserve on the southern shore of Mono Lake; Mono Lake Visitor's Center; Mono Lake Committee; Bodie State Park and Yosemite National Park, up and over the mountains on Highway 120 (closed in winter.)

Top, children stand beside the tufa towers along the shores of Mono Lake, the "dead sea" Twain wrote about in *Roughing It*. Bottom, the rough country near Monoville, California.

The black ring in the center of the photo are brine flies along the shores of Mono Lake. In the summer, millions of brine flies lay their eggs along Mono's shores. The Paiutes dried the pupae of the brine flies and made a meal of a sort. Surprisngly the food tasted somewhat good.

Monoville

Under favorable circumstances it snows at least once in every single month of the year, in the little town of Mono [Monoville.] So uncertain is the climate in summer that a lady who goes visiting cannot hope to be prepared for all emergencies unless she takes her fan under one arm and her snowshoes under the other.

Chapter 38 *Roughing It*

Sam Clemens passed through Monoville in August, 1862, with Cal Higbie, on their way to Trumboll Lake for trout fishing. Clemens at the time was prospecting and mining at Aurora, Nevada 25 miles east of Monoville.

The historic site of Monoville is located in the Eastern Sierra 1 mile east of Conway Summit on U.S. Highway 395, 12 miles south of Bridgeport and 13 miles north of Lee Vining, California. All that remains of Monoville are a stone cabin and scarred hillsides destroyed by hydraulic mining.

Monoville was the first major gold strike in the Eastern Sierra. Cord Norst discovered rich placer deposits at Monoville in the spring of 1859. Dick and Lee Vining, for whom nearby Lee Vining was named, were among the first Monoville miners.

The Monoville placer gold was easily recovered through washing. The best claims produced a pound of gold a day. At $14-15 an ounce, this amounted to a hefty sum at this time.

California miners from the western slope flocked to Monoville when the Sierra passes cleared in the spring of 1860. The camp quickly became the first major settlement east of the Sierra and south of Lake Tahoe. Monoville was soon built up during the summer of 1860 with several hotels, saloons, a Post Office and 40 houses, some two story. At its peak in the summer of 1860, Monoville had a population that varied between 500-2,000.

Monoville was primarily a placer mining site. Placer gold is loose gold that is separated from the dirt by various means of washing. One of the problems of mining the Monoville placer gold was the lack of water at the site. During the spring runoff, water was plentiful but with summer the slender creeks shrank and fights over water rights broke out.

To solve the water problem, water ditches were dug, one from Mill Creek, south of Monoville. A flume carried the water part way down the steep mountainsides. Remains of the flume can be seen today near Conway Summit.

When Aurora boomed in 1861, many of the Monoville miners moved on. But a few remained, and as late as 1864, Monoville was being considered as the Mono County seat.

After nearby Bodie boomed in 1878, Monoville received renewed attention. Hydraulic mining was introduced and huge hillsides were literally washed down by high pressured water hoses.

Though it had limited success, Monoville served as an important supply point for prospecting parties. All important later gold and silver discoveries including Bodie and Aurora were made by men who were supplied provisions at Monoville.

Long Valley

For more than two weeks I have been slashing around in the White Mountain District, partly for pleasure and partly for other reasons.

Sam Clemens in a letter to Orion Clemens, September 9, 1862

In August, 1862, while living and mining at Aurora, Nevada, Mark Twain took a "walking trip" of about 70 miles where he fished and hunted. This would have likely put him in the approximate area of Long Valley where the Owens River offered good fishing.

Long Valley is located in the Eastern Sierra of California half way between Bishop and Mammoth Lakes. Today a large portion of Long Valley is covered by Crowley Lake, a reservoir for the City of Los Angeles.

The Aurora to Owens Valley Road passed through Long Valley and crossed the mountains at Taylor Canyon. These mountains near Glass Mountain separate Long Valley from the Mono Basin. In the early 1860's, the Aurora to Owens Valley Road was used to haul supplies from nearby Owens Valley in the south to the silver mining town of Aurora northeast of Mono Lake. The narrow Owens River flowed through Long Valley and the trout fishing was good.

The Owens River and Long Valley, although 250 miles north of Los Angeles, became important to the growth of Los Angeles in the early part of this century. William Mulholland, Chief Engineer for the water department, had realized that without a significant new source of water, Los Angeles could not grow. The Los Angeles river and the wells and springs surrounding Los Angeles were unable to provide an adequate source of water. Mulholland began searching for a new source.

Fred Eaton, former mayor of Los Angeles, owned a large portion of property near the headwaters of the Owens River: Long Valley. Eaton and Mulholland were good friends. Eaton made Mulholland aware of the Owens River as a valuable source of water for the growing but thirsty city of Los Angeles. Mulholland visited and inspected the Owens Valley and the Owens River. He considered Long Valley, about 40 miles north of the Owens Valley, an ideal site for a dam and reservoir to hold the Owens River water.

Eaton was willing to sell Long Valley to Los Angeles for the right price. Unfortunately, Mulholland and Eaton could never agree on a suitable price and Long Valley became a wedge between the two friends that lasted for years and had drastic results for the farmers of the Owens Valley.

There were many rich farms and cattle ranches in the Owens Valley dependent on water from the Owens River. Disputes over water rights arose between the Owens Valley farmers and the City of Los Angeles. Rather than trying to reach an equitable solution for sharing the Owens River, Mulholland's answer to the prob-

lem was to put the squeeze on the Owens Valley Farmers.

Los Angeles began buying out the Owens Valley farms and did so ruthlessly and unfairly, checker-boarding the area, buying out one farmer, and leaving the next. This caused serious problems for the Owens Valley farmers who depended on cooperative irrigation ditches. Each farmer was responsible for keeping his portion of the irrigation ditches clear so that water could pass through the valley to all the farms. When one farmer was removed by the City, that left his portion of the ditch unattended and the water ditches became clogged. The City's checker-boarding plan, fouled the water ditches and angered and frustrated the Owens Valley farmers.

In the end, the Los Angeles Department of Water and Power (DWP) made it nearly impossible for the Owens Valley farms to survive.

A dam at Long Valley could have been the solution to sharing the waters of the Owens River. Enough water could have been stored in the dam to allow for the irrigation of the Owens Valley farms and for use in Los Angeles.

However, Fred Eaton and Mulholland could never settle on a fair price for the Long Valley dam site and the dam was not built until years after the Owens Valley farms had been destroyed by the City of Los Angeles.

In the late 1920's and 30's, Los Angeles instituted a complete buyout of most of the Owens Valley farmers. Today, Los Angeles owns most of Owens Valley. Much of the desert land that was claimed and turned into rich farms and cattle ranches by hardy pioneers, has been allowed by the City of Los Angeles to revert to desert. Many of the beautiful cottonwood trees the settlers planted, that beautified and gave shade in this desert valley, have been bulldozed or poisoned by the DWP. Farmhouses, barns, fences and ranches, were torn down or bulldozed by the DWP. One farmer said the valley looked like a war zone that had been obliterated by artillery after the DWP had gone through it.

The destruction of the Owens Valley settlements by the City of Los Angeles is one of the most tragic events in California history. It caused the California Legislature to publicly censure the City of Los Angeles in the 1920's.

The damage, destruction and ill will produced by the City of Los Angeles through greed and lack of compassion, continues to this day. [Editor's note: The author is currently writing a novel about the Owens Valley water war tentatively titled, *The Rape of Owens Valley*.]

Trumboll Lake

At the end of the week we adjourned to the Sierras on a fishing excursion, and spent several days in camp under snowy Castle Peak, and fished successfully for trout in a bright, miniature lake whose surface was between ten and eleven thousand feet above the level of the sea; cooling ourselves during the hot August noons by sitting on snowbanks ten feet deep, under whose sheltering edges fine grass and dainty flowers flourished luxuriously; and at night entertained ourselves by almost freezing to death.

Chapter 39 *Roughing It*

In August, 1862 Sam Clemens and Cal Higbie, who were mining at Aurora about 25 miles away, spent a week in the Sierra camping and fishing. In *Roughing It*, Twain wrote of this time, "...we adjourned to the Sierra on a fishing excursion, and spent several days in camp under snowy Castle Peak, and fished successfully for trout in a bright, miniature lake..." The author discovered that the "miniature lake" is Trumboll Lake. Today there is a nearby campground and the lake provides good fishing.

Trumboll Lake is located in the Eastern Sierra near Conway Summit between Bridgeport and Lee Vining. To reach the lake, take U.S. Highway 395 from Bridgeport, 13 miles to Conway Summit, then go west 5 miles on Virginia Lakes road. Or head north from Lee Vining 12 miles. The lake cannot be reached in winter as the road is not kept clear of snow.

Virginia Lakes road takes you high up into a narrow canyon with high, rocky mountains above. The area is only accessible in late spring, summer and early autumn. The canyon is particularly dangerous in winter because of avalanches. A couple years ago, an avalanche ripped down the mountain and mowed down a forest as if the timbers were blades of grass. Afterward, the area looked like something after an atomic blast. The trees lay flat and twisted.

There are several lakes in the area for fishing, campgrounds and the Virginia Lake Resort.

The surrounding area was prospected and mined after 1867. The Dunderberg Mine was the major development in the Castle Peak District. In July, 1867, Charles Snyder and Company sank a 40 foot shaft and hauled the ore to Aurora for milling. The ore assayed $50 a ton in gold and silver.

In 1870, Dr. George Munckton, a Carson City druggist, bought the Dunderberg claims but by 1872, he was bankrupt. The property was sold at a Sheriff's auction in 1872.

In 1878, A.K. Bryant and G.K. Porter bought the Dunderberg Mine and worked it until 1886 when water in the mines and the high altitude caused failure.

In 1891, English capitalists tried their hand; they re-timbered and laid new track in the tunnels but by 1903 they too gave up.

Trumboll Lake in the Eastern Sierra, below Castle Peak. Clemens and Cal Higbie fished and camped here in August, 1862. Mark Twain wrote about their pleasant excursion in *Roughing It*. Trumboll Lake is still a good place to fish just off Virginia Lakes Road near Conway Summit, south of Bridgeport, California.

Part 2

Local Reporter Becomes Mark Twain

Mark Twain about 1863 when he was reporting for the *Territorial Enterprise* in Virginia City, Nevada.

1

When Sam Clemens walked into Virginia City in the middle of September 1862, it was a child about three years old. The newly formed town was a hodgepodge of canvas tents, dugouts in the hillsides, stone cabins, frame cabins and one and two story frame buildings. The dirt streets were mud holes when it rained and dust bowls when the fierce Washoe zephyrs blew, clogged day and night with freight wagons, teams of horses, mules and men on horseback. One often risked his life attempting to cross the street. Until recently, supplies had been packed in on animals up the steep mountain paths. Finally a decent road was carved out of the mountain and wagons were able to make the grade. Badly needed supplies arrived, lumber, feed, mining supplies, vegetables and meat. The town flourished. It was filled with frenzied miners, speculators, businessmen and armed killers looking for their next victims. Three years earlier there had been nothing here but sagebrush, rock and a few pine nut trees. Now a great mining town was taking shape on a high, steep mountain side in the middle of nowhere.

Since the discovery of gold and silver in 1859, the Comstock mines have produced more than 400 million dollars. Their tremendous wealth helped the Union win the Civil War and financed the building of San Francisco. Sam Clemens arrived in mid-September just in time for the first big boom in 1863. Between 1863-67 the Comstock mines yielded 20 million dollars. During the spectacular "Bonanza" years, 1873-

Virginia City in the late 1870's looking west toward Mt. Davidson, the peak at the far upper right. The California Pan Mill is in the foreground. The white piles are mine tailings.

80, the Comstock mines produced more than 300 million dollars in gold and silver.

Virginia City eventually reached a population of 25,000 in the mid-1870's, crammed into a town about a mile square. Where other mining towns were wooden and men eked out a bare existence, much of Virginia City was brick. C Street became the main thoroughfare and central business district. On both sides were wooden and brick buildings, some five stories high. Here were located shops and businesses of every sort: grocery stores, meat markets, livery stables, saloons, brokerage houses, tailors, banks, jewelry stores, boarding houses, hotels and others. Stores were stocked with the best merchandise. You could find just about anything you wanted or needed. The town was cosmopolitan, rich and proud. Restaurants were the finest west of New York. Miners feasted on

well prepared, quality food from fresh oysters from San Francisco to prime rib; most restaurants had well stocked wine cellars.

Miners lived well and were paid well, earning $4-$6 a day, top pay for the time. In their off hours they filled the saloons where they misspent their hard earnings on whisky and gambling. When Mark Twain lived in Virginia City 1862-64, there were 51 saloons, over 100 during the extravagant 1870's. Miners consumed liquor in great quantities, mostly wine, beer and whisky. To relieve boredom and loneliness, they found amusement in the three redlight districts, dance halls, hurdy gurdy houses and at Piper's and Maguire's opera houses where traveling actors and musicians entertained.

For twenty years Virginia City's silver mines were known throughout America. For fifteen years they affected the lives of Americans everywhere, sometimes remotely sometimes directly with the rise and fall of mining stocks. Virginia City became an illusive Promised Land for thousands who believed their fortunes could be made over night. Some lives, like Mark

The International Hotel in the 1860's on the northwest corner of C and Union streets. This was one of Twain's haunts. He and Dan De Quille roomed together in the Meyers Building on B Street. The building no longer stands.

Twain's, became wonderful rags-to-riches stories. But many did not do so well; there are many tales of terrible tragedies.

When Sam Clemens arrived in Virginia City, he was twenty-six, to turn twenty-seven November 30. He stood 5 feet, 8 1/2 inches and weighed about 145 pounds. His body was small and slender yet his head seemed almost too large. "His head was striking," Bret Harte wrote. "He had the curly hair, the aquiline nose, and even the aquiline eye—an eye so eagle-like that a second lid would not have surprised me..." Out of this unusual head two piercing eyes dissected the world and the creatures God had placed in it. His eyes were commanding, magnetic, strong yet soft. They caught one's attention, possessed "a calm, penetrating, unwavering gaze," thought George Ade. They seemed wise beyond their years. To William Dean Howells, a friend of over forty years, Clemens' eyes were greenish-blue. To Susy Clemens, her father's eyes were blue but to James Fields his eyes were gray. Clemens' eyes likely changed with his moods or with lighting. Dark bushy eyebrows gave his face a serious, meditative appearance. For all his humor, Clemens seldom smiled. This striking head was ornamented with a thick crop of curly, mahogany hair. Clemens in Virginia City at first oiled his hair and combed it back. In time he dispensed with the oil; his hair grew long and wild and took on the rugged, youthful appearance by which the world later recognized him.

Once he shaved his prospector's beard, Clemens fair skinned face was revealed. His face seemed both delicate and rugged, his mouth, "as delicate as a woman's," Kipling wrote. He had not yet grown the thick, bushy mustache which would define his face a lifetime.

Though his face conveyed strength and intelligence, his small body at times appeared helpless. It was not the body of a laborer but that of a thinker. Joe Goodman thought Clemens' bodily helplessness belied his great mental capacity. Clemens nearly died as a feeble infant; as an adult he was susceptible to respiratory illnesses, bronchitis, severe colds. His hands were small and delicate, calloused from his mining labors in Aurora.

"His dress was careless, and his general manner one of supreme indifference to surroundings and circumstances," thought Bret Harte. He seemed to some as if he was not at all there, that his mind was somewhere else, on a plain normal humans do not visit. This caused him to be absent minded, at times careless in his dress. William Dean Howells said Clemens, "was apt to smile into your face with a subtle but amiable perception, and yet with a sort of remote absence; you were all there for him, but he was not all there for you."

In his mouth at every waking hour was a cigar or a pipe. Clemens literally lived in a cloud of tobacco smoke and loved the smell; this was Paradise. He had smoked since a boy and now smoked incessantly. Years later he said of his smoking, "Me, who never learned to smoke, but always smoked; me, who came into this world asking for a light... Why, my old boy, when they used to tell me I would shorten my life ten years by smoking... they little knew how trivial and valueless I would regard a decade that had no smoking in it!" *Enterprise* staff dubbed his pipe, "The Remains" and "The Pipe of a thousand Smells."

Clemens moved slowly. To some he seemed lazy. *Enterprise* editor Joe Goodman thought he was, "kind of lazy or slow in his movements." To Rollin Daggett, assistant editor, he was "slothful." His strong Missouri drawl inherited from his mother, made Clemens seem that much slower. Susy Clemens said her father lost his drawl in private. Clemens apparently capitalized on his drawl which gave his speech a folksy down to earth tone.

Clemens readily admitted he hated physical labor. "I do not like to work even when another person does it." Clemens often spoke of himself as being lazy. Once while looking through the writings of Suetonius he found a reference to a Flavius Clemens, a man widely known "for his want of energy." Twain wrote in the margin, "I guess this is where our line starts." Clemens was not lazy; he detested drudgery. Clemens put his all into whatever he loved or enjoyed. Once he was committed to a project he worked steadily until the job was completed. He possessed extraordinary tenacity and energy. He spent eight years off and on writing *Huckleberry Finn* ; over his lifetime he wrote and rewrote by hand volumes of literature. Though *Enterprise* editor Rollin Daggett said Clemens gave fellow reporter Dan De Quille all the dirty work, De Quille said he and Clemens agreed to divide the work load. De Quille wrote pieces which required attention to detail and numbers, usually dealing with technical aspects of mining activities. Clemens, on the other hand, was best suited for human interest stories.

One of Clemens' outstanding characteristics was the ease with which he made friends. Clemens was a human magnet and drew people to him naturally. He did not have to work to get the attention of others. Joe Goodman said, "Back in the old days Sam was the best company, the drollest entertainer and the most interesting fellow imaginable. His humor was always cropping out..." Those who knew Clemens best, said his speech was funnier than his writing. Clemens would tell humorous stories for hours while an enraptured gathering laughed till their sides ached and time seemed to pass quickly. Clemens enjoyed being the center of attention and he was skillful in the ways he achieved it. He was a ham, an actor, a born entertainer. He enjoyed people, enjoyed himself and loved making people laugh and feel good.

His speech was disarming, frank and unpretentious. He could talk for hours over a wide spectrum of subjects. Conversation stimulated him but he was a better talker than a listener. His speech, especially during the Western years, was often profane. Intimates accepted his profanity, at times wondered at his skill. Katy

Maguire's Opera House in the 1860's is the two story building just right of the flag pole. Mark Twain gave one of his first lectures here. The building no longer stands.

Leary, Twain's longtime housekeeper said, "It was sort of funny, and part of him some how. Sort of amusing it was—and gay—not like real swearing." Others said Clemens' profane outrages were performances not to be missed. Once in a letter to Howells, Twain attacked an enemy as a "quadrilateral, astronomical, incandescent son-of-a-bitch;" another he called a "Damn half-developed fetus!"

Clemens, even during his lectures, spoke in a low, conversational voice but when angered, he lost his drawl, spoke rapidly, and his voice rose in pitch to an acid whine.

Clemens enjoyed playing the mischievous prankster. He often played practical jokes on *Enterprise* friends though he hated practical jokes played on himself. To many, Clemens

was a lovable scoundrel whom they easily forgave. Senator William "Bill" Stewart, who knew Clemens well in Virginia City and later in Washington, D.C., said Clemens was, "the most lovable scamp and nuisance who ever blighted Nevada." Clemens while working for the *Enterprise* enjoyed creating news, generally in the form of imaginative stories about people he knew or did not know. Stewart in his *Reminiscences* recalled Clemens the rascal in Virginia City:

Sam Clemens was a busy person. He went around putting things in the paper about people, and stirring up trouble. He did not care whether the things he wrote were true or not, just so he could write something, and naturally he was not popular. I did not associate with him.

This Clemens one day wrote something about a distinguished citizen of Virginia City, a friend of mine, which was entirely characteristic of Clemens, as it had not the slightest foundation in fact. I

The stagecoaches are in front of the office of Shaw's Fast Freight Line on C Street in Virginia City. Mark Twain rode these stages back and forth to Carson City.

remonstrated with him.

"You are getting worse every day," I said. "Why can't you be genial, like your brother Orion? You ought to be hung for what you have published this morning."

"I don't mean anything by that," returned Clemens. "I do not know this friend of yours. For all I am aware he may be a very desirable and conscientious man. But I must make a living, and so I must write. My employers demand it, and I am helpless..."

Clemens had a great habit of making fun of the young fellows and the girls, and wrote ridiculous pieces about parties and other social events, to which he was never invited. After a while he went over to Carson City, and touched up the people over there, and got everybody down on him. I thought he had faded from our midst forever, but the citizens of

Carson drove him away. At any rate, he drifted back to Virginia City in a few weeks. He didn't have a friend, but the boys got together and said they would give a party, and invite Clemens to it, and make him feel at home, and respectable and decent, and kindly, and generous, and loving, and considerate of the feelings of others. I could have warned them but I didn't.

Clemens went to that party and danced with the prettiest girls, and monopolized them, and enjoyed himself, and made a good meal, and then shoved over to the Enterprise *office and wrote the whole thing up in an outrageous manner. He lambasted that party for all the English language would allow, and if any of the guests was unfortunate enough to be awkward or had big feet, or a wart on the nose, Clemens did not forget it. He fairly strained his memory...*

After that he drifted away, and I thought he had been hanged, or elected to congress, or something like that, and I had forgotten him... I was confident that he would come to no good end, but I have heard of him from time to time since then, and I understand that he has settled down and become respectable.

Stewart and Clemens were friends. Stewart wrote the above piece years after Twain made fun of him in *Roughing It* and I imagine Stewart, as much a prankster as Clemens, enjoyed his opportunity to get back at Clemens for embarrassing him. Clemens was never chased out of Carson City as Stewart wrote. He was popular and had many friends. True, he wrote items from time to time which embarrassed people; but they were generally written in fun and the rough humor was appreciated by Comstockers. Of course, if a victim was an enemy, well, he deserved what he got.

Twain approached Stewart in the fall of 1867 while writing *The Innocents Abroad.* Twain needed a place to write and a temporary job. Stewart offered to share his apartment with Twain in Washington, D.C., where Twain wrote parts of *The Innocents Abroad.* Twain worked part-time as Stewart's private secretary, a job he did not relish and which caused kindly Bill Stewart no end of grief.

Twain in, "My Late Senatorial Secretaryship," tells something of the problem Stewart had to deal with:

My employer sent for me one morning tolerably early... There was something portentous in his appearance. His cravat was untied, his hair was in a state of disorder, and his countenance bore about it signs of a suppressed storm. He held a package of letters in his tense grasp, and I knew that the dreaded Pacific mail was in. He said:

"I thought you were worthy of confidence." I said, "Yes, sir."

He said, "I gave you a letter from certain of my constituents in the State of Nevada, asking the establishment of a post office at Baldwin's Ranch, and told you to answer it, as ingeniously as you could, with arguments which should persuade them that there was no real necessity for an office at that place."

I felt easier. "Oh, if that is all, sir I did do that."
"Yes, you did. I will read your answer for your own humiliation:

" 'Washington, Nov. 24.

Gentlemen: What the mischief do you suppose you want with a post-office at Baldwin's Ranch? It would not do you any good. If any letters came there, you couldn't read them, you know; and, besides, such letters as ought to pass through, with money in them, for other localities, would not be likely to get through, you must perceive at once; and that would make trouble for us all. No, don't bother about a post-office in your camp. I have your best interests at heart, and feel that it would only be ornamental folly. What you want is a nice jail, you know—a nice, substantial jail and a free school. These will be a lasting benefit to you. These will make you really contented and happy. I will move in the matter at once.

Very truly, etc.,
Mark Twain,
*For James W.N. **, U.S. Senator.' "*

"That is the way you answered that letter. Those people say they will hang me, if I ever enter that district again; and I am perfectly satisfied they will, too."
"Well, sir, I did not know I was doing any harm. I only wanted to convince them."
"Ah. Well, you did convince them, I make no manner of doubt. Now, here is another specimen..."

Clemens enjoyed upsetting and shocking people. This was his idea of fun. Clemens *was* Tom Sawyer, a boy who never grew up. Howells, who knew Clemens extraordinarily well, said, "He was a youth to the end of his days, the heart of a boy with the head of sage; the heart of a good boy, or a bad boy, but always a willful boy, and willfullest to show himself out at every time for just the boy he was."

Clemens remained youthful until his death. He skipped up steps, leapfrogged on the floor.

1925

Mark Twain's desk at the *Territorial Enterprise* in Virginia City.

He was led by his emotions, always spontaneous, at times impulsive. He defied authority and was willfully independent. He was eager, intense, prone to extremes in moods, one moment high and happy, the next, low and depressed. He had extreme reactions of glory and despair, praise and condemnation. He loved pageantry and parades, children and animals, the cat his favorite. Once while staying with Tom Fitch and his family at Washoe City, near Virginia City, Clemens insisted that Jim, the Fitch's Maltese cat, sleep with him every night.

Clemens was always raving about one fad or another. He loved bright colors, red, his favorite and later insisted his billiard table have red felt instead of green. He enjoyed pranks and shocking people by outrageous dress. Clemens once showed up at a dance in Gold Hill wearing white pants, huge buffalo shoes and yellow kid gloves. And he enjoyed games, billiards, poker and euchre his favorites in his mining camp days.

When Clemens died at seventy-four, Katy Leary said, "It was a terrible, cruel thing for him to die, really, because he was too young—that is, he felt young, you know, and that made him young..."

2

Some time during the first two weeks of September, 1862, Clemens finally showed up at the *Territorial Enterprise.* The *Enterprise* was then located at 27 North C Street next to the Wells Fargo offices where the Silver Queen Casino stands today. Clemens may have first roomed in the *Enterprise* offices or with a friend. Later he lodged at Mrs. Williamson's White House boarding house on South C Street. His neighbors were Clement Rice, a reporter for the Virginia *Union,* who became a best friend and William Gillespie, who reported for the *Enterprise* and became first clerk for the Territorial Legislature.

Left, the *Territorial Enterprise* Building in Virginia City where Mark Twain worked from August, 1863 to May, 1864. Right, the Silver Queen Saloon stands on the site of the previous *Enterprise* office.

After his hard times at Aurora, Virginia City was more to Clemens' liking. The roaring mining town offered Clemens the same breadth of life as the larger Mississippi River towns he was familiar with and enjoyed. Though Virginia City was not on a waterway and small, it was cosmopolitan and provided Clemens with the variety and wild times he craved. Here were many people from many nations working, living, playing, going about their business. Where life at Aurora was dull and hard, life in Virginia City was easy and invigorating. At Aurora Clemens had lived in crude shelters and it was

often cold. In Virginia City Clemens had a warm room, 15 restaurants to choose from and 51 saloons to drink and socialize in. Clemens was back in the active social life he enjoyed.

Clemens returned to the familiar turf on the *Enterprise.* The odor of ink, the ticking of the compositors at work, the sound of scribbling quills, the rattling of the printing presses, were all familiar and comfortable and a part of his youth. But now Clemens held a more important position: he created the copy the compositors set and the printing presses manufactured.

Clemens at first felt unsure in his new role as local reporter. There were times he felt like backing out. But when the thought of unemployment and dependency struck, he decided "necessity is the mother of taking chances."

Sam approached Joe Goodman and asked what he should do. Goodman replied:

The steam powered presses in the press room of the *Territorial Enterprise.* They are still located in the basement of the *Enterprise* Building on C Street.

...go all over town and ask all sorts of questions, make notes of the information gained, and write them out for publication. And he added:

"Never say 'We learn' so-and so or 'It is reported,' or 'It is rumored,' or 'We understand' so-and so, but go to headquarters and get the absolute facts, and then speak and say "It is so-and so, 'Otherwise, people will not put confidence in your news. Unassailable certainty is the thing that gives a newspaper the firmest and most valuable reputation."

It was the whole thing in a nutshell; and to this day, when I find a reporter commencing his article with "We understand," I gather a suspicion that he has not taken as much pains to inform himself as he ought to have done. I moralize well, but I did not always practice well when I was a city editor; I let fancy get the upper hand of fact too often when there was dearth of news. I can never forget my first day's experience as a reporter. I wandered about town questioning everybody, and finding out that nobody

knew anything. At the end of five hours my notebook was still barren. I spoke to Mr. Goodman. He said:

"Dan used to make a good thing out of the hay wagons in a dry time when there were no fires or inquests. Are there no hay-wagons in from Truckee? If there are, you might speak of the renewed activity and all that sort of thing, in the hay business, you know. It isn't sensational or exciting, but it fills up and looks business-like."

I canvassed the city again and found one wretched old hay-truck dragging in from the country. But I made affluent use of it. I multiplied it by sixteen, brought it into town from sixteen different directions, made sixteen separate items of it, and got up such another sweat about hay as Virginia City had ever seen in the world before.

This was encouraging. Two nonpareil columns had to be filled, and I was getting along. Presently, when things began to look dismal again, a desperado killed a man in a saloon and joy returned once more. I never was so glad over any mere trifle before in my life. I said to the murderer:

"Sir, you are a stranger to me, but you have done me a kindness this day which I can never forget. If

The "Composing Room" inside the *Enterprise* Building. Here typesetters set the type by hand using metal letters.

whole years of gratitude can be to you any slight compensation, they shall be yours. I was in trouble and you have relieved me nobly and at a time when all seemed dark and drear. Count me your friend from this time forth, for I am not a man to forget a favor."

If I did not really say that to him I at least felt a sort of itching desire to do it. I wrote up the murder with a hungry attention to details, and when it was finished I experienced but one regret—namely, that they had not hanged my benefactor on the spot, so that I could work him up too.

Next I discovered some emigrant wagons going into camp on the plaza and I found that they had lately come through the hostile Indian country and had fared rather roughly. I made the best of the item that the circumstances permitted, and felt that if I were not confined with rigid limits by the presence of the reporters of the other papers I could add particulars that would make the article much more interesting. However, I found one wagon that was

going to California, and made some judicious inquiries of the proprietor. When I learned, through his short and surly answers to my cross-questioning, that he was certainly going on and would not be in the city next day to make trouble, I got ahead of the other papers, for I took down his list of names and added his party to the killed and wounded. Having more scope here, I put this wagon through an Indian fight that to this day has no parallel in history.

My two columns were filled. When I read them over in the morning I felt that I had found my legitimate occupation at last. I reasoned within myself that news, and stirring news, too, was what a paper needed, and I felt that I was peculiarly endowed with the ability to furnish it. Mr. Goodman said that I was as good a reporter as Dan. I desired no higher commendation. With encouragement like that, I felt I could take my pen and murder all the emigrants on the plains if need be, and the interests of the paper demanded it.

Chapter 42 *Roughing It*

Whether or not Clemens put the emigrants through an "Indian fight that to this day has no parallel in history," we cannot be certain. Only

Joe Goodman, editor and co-owner of the *Territorial Enterprise* and Mark Twain's friend. This photo was taken about the time Goodman was running the *Enterprise* in Virginia City in the late 1860's.

a scattering of early *Enterprise* issues survive; this article is not among existing issues. It is true, while reporting for the *Enterprise*, Clemens exaggerated events to make his articles more entertaining. He, Bill Stewart and others testify of his skill at avoiding facts.

However, one of Clemens' first hoaxes written for the *Enterprise* has survived, the "Petrified Man," published October 4, 1862. With the seriousness of Job, Clemens told unsuspecting readers of a petrified man discovered at Grav-

elly Ford near the Humboldt Mining District about 200 miles northeast of Virginia City. In part it read:

Every limb and feature of the stone mummy was perfect, not even excepting the left leg, which had evidently been a wooden one during the lifetime of the owner—which lifetime, by the way, came to a close about a century ago, in the opinion of a savant who has examined the defunct. The body was in a sitting posture, and leaning against a huge mass of croppings; the attitude was pensive, the right thumb rested against the side of the nose; the left thumb partially supported the chin, the forefinger pressing the inner corner of the eye, and drawing it partly open; the right eye was closed, and the fingers of the right hand spread out. This strange freak of nature

From left to right William Gillespie, Charles Parker, Dan De Quille (William Wright), Robert Lowery and Alf. Doten, all Comstock journalists and friends of Mark Twain.

created a profound sensation in the vicinity.

Clemens added that a coroner's inquest superintended by "Justice Sewell or Sowell" concluded the "deceased came to his death from protracted exposure." When citizens offered to give the body a decent burial by blasting the man from his limestone seat, the judge declared that the desecration would be a "little less than sacrilege."

Not content to allow the article to do its damage, the following day, Clemens pressed the hoax further:

Mr. Herr Weisnicht has just arrived in Virginia City from the Humboldt mines and regions beyond. He brings with him the head and foot of the petrified man, lately found in the mountains near Gravelly Ford. A skillful assayer has analyzed a small portion of the dirt found under the nail of the great toe and pronounces the man to have been a native of the Kingdom of New Jersey. As a trace of "speculation" is still discernible in the left eye, it is thought the man was on his way to what is now the Washoe mining region [northwestern Nevada] for the purpose of locating the Comstock. The remains brought in are to be seen in a neat glass case in the third story of the Library Building, where they have been temporarily placed by Mr. Weisnicht for the inspection of the curious, and where they may be examined by any one who will take the trouble to visit them.

Mark Twain, years later explained why he wrote the "Petrified Man."

...In the fall of 1862, in Nevada and California, the people got to running wild about extraordinary petrifications and other natural marvels...This mania was becoming a little ridiculous... I felt called upon to destroy this growing evil...

I had a temporary falling out with Mr._____, the new coroner and justice of the peace of Humboldt, and thought I might as well touch him up a little at the same time and make him ridiculous, and thus combine pleasure with business. So I told, in patient belief-compelling detail, all about the finding of a petrified man at Gravelly Ford (exactly a hundred and twenty miles... from where _____ lived); how all the savants of the immediate neighborhood had been to examine it... how those savants all pronounced the petrified man to have been in a state of complete petrification for over ten generations; and then, with a seriousness that I ought to have been ashamed to assume, I stated that as soon as Mr. _____ heard the news he summoned a jury, mounted his mule, and posted off, with noble reverence for official duty, on that awful five days journey, through alkali, sagebrush, peril of body, and imminent starvation, to hold an inquest on this man that had been dead and turned to everlasting stone for more than three hundred years!...

From beginning to end the "Petrified Man" squib was a string of roaring absurdities, albeit they were told with an unfair pretense of truth that even... I was in some danger of believing my own fraud. But I really had no desire to deceive anybody, and no expectation of doing it... But I was too ingenious...

As a satire on the petrification mania... my Petrified Man was a disheartening failure; for everybody received him in innocent good faith...

Sketches New and Old

The "Petrified Man" was printed by other Western papers. Most readers accepted the article as fact.

Clemens intended the "Petrified Man" to embarrass Coroner Sewell of Humboldt mining district with whom Clemens was angry. Sewell had apparently refused to forward details regarding recent deaths. Clemens succeeded in embarrassing Sewell who reportedly received hundreds of inquiries about the mysterious petrified man. Clemens, true to his nature, had gotten revenge, "I could not have gotten more real comfort out of him without killing him," Mark Twain later wrote.

The "Petrified Man" was the first Western article Clemens used to satirize human stupidity. It was the first of many articles Clemens

wrote to embarrass men with who odds or whose motives he disappr

The *Enterprise* staff was a close fraternity of intelligent, young bachelors—nearly all in their mid-twenties, except for Dan De Quille who was in his early thirties and married (his wife and family lived in Iowa.) The men worked and played together. After the paper went to press at two in the morning, the staff and the compositors gathered in the composing room, drank beer and sang the popular war songs of the day until dawn.

Clemens' life fell into a routine. He stayed up late, often until dawn, went to bed in the early morning hours, waking around eleven or twelve. After a large breakfast of steak and eggs, lots of coffee, pie or cake, he roamed the town spending much time in the saloons where men gathered and news was easy to find. If there was a new strike in one of the mines, he, along with Dan De Quille, the chief mining reporter, went to inspect. There were frequent murders and fights and while reporting on one, another would break out. There were the usual trips to the police station to gather details of recent crimes. The local stock exchange was a good place to find news; it was always busy.

The life of a roaming reporter suited Clemens well. He enjoyed mixing with people; he was interested in learning what others knew. He was full of nervous energy and enjoyed movement, though trudging up and down Virginia City's steep streets probably became a chore. As time passed, Clemens became more of a local columnist than news reporter. In such a close knit community as Virginia City, Clemens' magnetic personality was noticed.

As a member of the *Enterprise* staff, he was one of a select elite. There were free passes to shows, complimentary drinks and free dinners for plugging local businesses in his column. In return for mentioning their mines in the *Enterprise,* mine owners gave Clemens hundreds of dollars in free mining stocks, some useless, some quite valuable which Clemens traded or

Left to right, the "Three Saints" Artemus Ward (Charles Farrar Browne), Dan De Quille and Mark Twain.

sold. Clemens earned twenty-five dollars a week, an excellent salary at that time, five dollars a week more than miners made risking their necks in dangerous mines. With so much given him plus his high salary, Clemens was living high after his hard times at Aurora.

Clemens spent late afternoons and evenings writing at the long table at the *Enterprise* offices. When he finished an article, Dan read it over or Clemens passed it to Rollin Daggett, assistant editor. When an article was approved, Clemens handed it to the compositor who hand set each word with individual metal letters in large wooden cases used to print the newspaper.

Dan De Quille, then the local reporter and editor, stayed with the paper until mid-November teaching Clemens the ropes. Goodman had hired Clemens to replace De Quille who was taking a vacation to visit his wife and family in Iowa. De Quille would return to Vir-

ginia City at the end of July, 1863.

Virginia City was then a twenty-four hour town. After the paper was put to bed, the *Enterprise* boys made rounds to saloons and restaurants. Some of their favorite saloons were John Piper's Old Corner Saloon in the basement of his Opera House at the corner of B and Union; Tom Peaseley's Sazerac Saloon at 10 South C Street near Union; Almack's, The International Hotel, The Delta Saloon and when Maguire's Opera House opened, the boys met at the Branch Saloon. Favorite restaurants were the Chauvel House Restaurant at 12 North C Street, Delmonico's at 32 and 34 South C Street between Union and Taylor, the Eagle Restaurant and Barnum's at the corner of B and Sutton. For entertainment there were shows at Piper's Opera House, later Maguire's; there were dance hall's and hurdy gurdy girls and of course, many prostitutes. Though De Quille and other journalists visited the redlight districts, there is no evidence Clemens did. Clemens, a billiards fanatic, probably spent considerable time at the Bank Exchange Billiard Saloon at 5 North B Street.

...Science is a very pleasant subject to dilate upon, and we consider that we are as able to dilate upon it as any man that walks—but if we have been guilty of carelessness in any part of this article, so that our method of assaying as set forth herein may chance to differ from Mr. Theall's, we would advise that gentleman to stick to his own plan nevertheless, and not go to following ours—His is as good as any known to science. If we have struck anything new in our method, however, we shall be happy to hear of it, so that we can take steps to secure ourself the benefits accruing therefrom.

In mid-November, Joe Goodman sent Clemens to Carson City to report on the second Territorial Legislature which met mid-November through December. Sam stayed in Carson City at Orion's house with his brother, his wife, Mollie and their seven year old daughter, Jennie. This house still stands and is located at the northwest corner of Spear and Division streets at 502 N. Division.

As Secretary of Nevada Territory, Orion Clemens was second in command to Governor Nye. Orion was acting governor when Nye was out of the Territory which was frequent. As brother to the acting Governor and legislative reporter for the most powerful voice in the Territory, Clemens was someone to be reckoned with. Though politics and bureaucratic shuffling bored Clemens, he enjoyed making fun of politicians who took themselves too seriously and legislative bills that made no sense.

For six weeks, Clemens attended the daily legislative meetings at the Warm Springs Hotel, today the Nevada State Penitentiary on east Fifth Street. Abe Curry had kindly donated his hotel as a place for legislators to meet.

After legislative meetings, reporters and representatives met in the Carson saloons.

Clement Rice, Clemens' boarding house neighbor and reporter for the Virginia *Union*, also attended the legislative meetings. Rice was an experienced legislative reporter. After read-

Rollin M. Daggett Mark Twain's managing editor while he reported for the *Enterprise*. Daggett taught Twain to attack injustice.

Clemens was in best form writing human interest stories where he was free to interpret events in his own humorous way. He enjoyed writing about people and he was aware that readers liked reading about people. He did not enjoy reporting which required him to carefully note numbers, measurements and solid facts and made no attempt to hide his preference. Once while describing the assaying process, he went along fairly well until the end when he apologized for half-remembering some of the process "owing to lager beer." He concluded the article with:

ing one of Clemens' reports in the *Enterprise*, Rice published a column ridiculing Clemens' political naiveté. Clemens bounced back with a stunning rebuttal calling Rice's reports unreliable. This began a series of editorial battles between Clemens and Rice. The attacks were made in fun; Clemens and Rice were good friends and later traveled to San Francisco together. The bantering at times was hilarious. Clemens repeatedly referred to Rice as the "Unreliable" and the name stuck. Clemens depicted the Unreliable as a seedy drunk who was forever borrowing money for drinks. Western newspapers followed the bantering between the rival reporters with interest:

...This poor miserable outcast, crowded himself into the Firemen's Ball night before last, and glared upon the happy scene with his evil eye for a few minutes. He had his coat buttoned up to his chin, which is the way he always does when he has no shirt on. As soon as the management found out he was there, they put him out, of course. They had better have allowed him to stay, though, for he walked straight across the street, with all his vicious soul

aroused, and climbed in at the back window of the supper room and gobbled up the last crumb of the repast provided for the guests, before he was discovered. This accounts for the scarcity of provisions at the Firemen's supper that night. Then he went home and wrote a particular description of our ball costume with his usual meanness, as if such information could be of any consequence to the public. He never vouchsafed a single compliment to our dress, either, after all the care and taste we had bestowed upon it. We despise that man.

On another occasion Clemens wrote an obituary for the Unreliable. The Unreliable, he wrote,

became a newspaper reporter, and crushed Truth to earth and kept her there; he bought and sold his own notes, and never paid his board; he pretended great friendship for Gillespie [clerk of the first Territorial Legislature] in order to get to sleep with him; then he took advantage of his bed fellow and robbed him of his glass eye and false teeth; of course he sold the articles, and Gillespie was obliged to issue more county scrip than the law allowed, in order to get them back again; the Unreliable broke into my trunk

Top left, Clement Rice, the "Unreliable," Twain's friend and roommate. Top right, William "Bill" Stewart, an attorney and Twain's friend. Bottom left, the grave of Nick Ambrose in the Empire Cemetery east of Carson City. Ambrose's place was allegedly the setting for the "Massacre at Dutch Nick's." Bottom right, John Piper who built three opera houses in Virginia City. He ran the Old Corner Saloon where Clemens was dubbed "Mark Twain" by friends.

Piper's Opera House in Virginia City today. This is the third version. The two previous opera houses burned down. On this site Twain gave one of his first lecture performances.

at Washoe City, and took jewelry and fine clothes and things, worth thousands and thousands of dollars; he was present, without invitation at every party and ball and wedding which transpired in Carson during thirteen years... He is dead and buried now, though, let him rest, let him rot...

P.S. By private letters from Carson, since the above was in type, I am pained to learn that the Unreliable, true to his unnatural instincts, came to life again in the midst of his funeral sermon, and remains so to this moment. He was always unreliable in life—he could not even be depended upon in death. The shrouded corpse shoved the coffin lid to one side, rose to a sitting position, cocked his eye at the minister and smiling said, "O let up...loan me two bits!" The frightened congregation rushed from the house, and the Unreliable followed them, with his coffin on his shoulder. He sold it for two dollars

and a half, and got drunk at a "bit house" [low class saloon] *on the proceeds. He is still drunk.*

Each Sunday Clemens wrote a dispatch from Carson City which summarized the week's political events. In the dispatch of January 31, 1863, Clemens for the first time signed it "Mark Twain." There was no fanfare, no beating drums, just "Mark Twain" signed to a weekly report in an isolated region of America. For the next seventeen months in Nevada, Clemens was known as the writer and the person Mark Twain.

Twain's work as a reporter for the *Territorial Enterprise* met several needs and made the job, at least in Virginia City, well suited for him: It enabled him to interact with people of all classes, from the rich banker to the hard rock miner. Gathering news and gossip appealed to his curiosity and his need for new experiences. Most importantly, writing a column each day for the local paper offered him the opportunity to test his humorous writing on an audience. The response was encouraging; in Virginia City

Mark Twain won his first notoriety as a humorous writer.

3

Mark Twain published his most well known story for the *Enterprise* October 28, 1863. It was an awful tale of murder and violence. The story first stunned readers; then it made them angry. It has since been called the "Massacre at Dutch Nick's" and this story, more than any other piece of Twain's *Enterprise* writing, made Mark Twain known to Western readers.

Mark Twain told unsuspecting readers,

...P. Hopkins or Philip Hopkins, has been residing with his family in the old log house just at the edge of the great pine forest which lies between Empire City and Dutch Nick's. The family consisted of 9 children—5 girls and 4 boys—the oldest of the group, Mary, being 19 years old, and the youngest, Tommy, about a year and a half...

...About 10 o'clock on Monday evening Hopkins dashed into Carson on horseback, with his throat cut from ear to ear, and bearing in his hand a reeking scalp from which the warm, smoking blood was still dripping, and fell in a dying condition in front of the Magnolia saloon. Hopkins expired in the course of five minutes, without speaking. The long red hair of the scalp he bore marked it as that of Mrs. Hopkins. A number of citizens, headed by Sheriff Gasherie, mounted at once and rode down to Hopkins' house, where a ghastly scene met their gaze. The scalpless corpse of Mrs. Hopkins lay across the threshold, with her head split open and her right hand almost severed from the wrist. Near her lay the ax which the murderous deed had been committed. In one of the bedrooms six of the children were found, one in bed and the others scattered about the floor. They were all dead. Their brains had evidently been dashed out with a club, and every mark about them seemed to have been made with a blunt instrument. The children must have struggled hard for their lives, as articles of their clothing and broken furniture were strewn about the room in the utmost confusion. Julia and Emma, aged...14 and 17, were found in the kitchen, Bruised and insensible, but it is thought the recovery is possible...

...Hopkins...had been a heavy owner in the best mines of Virginia and Gold Hill, but when the San Francisco papers exposed the game of cooking dividends in order to bolster up our stocks he grew afraid and sold out, and invested to an immense amount in the Spring Valley Water Company of San Francisco. He was advised to do this by a relative of his, one of the editors of the San Francisco Bulletin...

Shortly after Hopkins had invested all his capital in Spring Valley Water Company,

several dividends were cooked on this...property...Spring Valley stock went down to nothing...It is presumed that this misfortune drove him mad and resulted in his killing himself and the greater portion of his family.

Newspapers up and down the Pacific Coast immediately reprinted the story believing it was true. The next day Mark Twain published a single line, "I take it all back.—Twain"

Immediately, editors and readers throughout the West attacked Mark Twain and the *Enterprise* for publishing the gruesome hoax. The Reese River *Reveille* wrote, "Some of the papers are expressing astonishment that 'Mark Twain'...should perpetrate such a 'sell' as 'A Bloody Massacre Near Carson'...They don't know him. We would not be surprised at ANYTHING done by that silly idiot." Another wrote, "The ass who originated the story doubtless thinks he is old smarty'—we don't." The Virginia *Evening Bulletin* said of the "Massacre,"

...Now in the item referred to, there is not a particle of truth, but unfortunately people at a distance may not be able to detect the self contradictions that are all through this extraordinary item, and will probably consider this wholesale murder as an "o'er true tale." God knows our Territory has a reputation of being the theater of scenes of blood and violence that really do occur bad enough to satisfy our bitterest enemies. There does not exist any need to paint our characters any blacker than they really are. Those

who have ever been in the Territory will well know that Dutch Nick's and Empire City are one and the same place, nor is there any log cabin, nor any family of nine children of the name of Hopkins living there, or ever did live there. The whole story is as baseless as the fabric of a dream.

October 28, 1863

Mark Twain had not intended to mislead the public. He meant the "Massacre" to be taken as a satire. Apparently, he had written about the murders too convincingly and graphically. He had intended the story to do several things: reveal the devious practice of falsely inflating stock prices, embarrass San Francisco papers who should have warned the public about such schemes and to embarrass Pete Hopkins, of the Magnolia Saloon in Carson City, who had offended Twain in some way.

Mark Twain placed his real message at the end of the article. But readers either did not read this portion or missed the point. Twain wrote:

...The newspapers of San Francisco permitted this water company to go on borrowing money and cooking dividends, under cover of which cunning financiers crept out of the tottering concern, leaving the crash to come upon poor and unsuspecting stockholders, without offering to expose the villainy at work. We hope the fearful massacre detailed above may prove the saddest result of their silence.

Twain was stunned when local readers took the story seriously. He believed the details of the murder made it obvious that it was all a satire. Nor did he think newspapers outside the area would publish the story. He later wrote:

...The murderer was perfectly well known to every creature in the land as a bachelor, and consequently he could not murder his wife and nine children; ...there was not a "great pine forest between Empire City and Dutch Nick's," there wasn't a solitary tree within fifteen miles of either place; and, finally, it

was...notorious that Empire City and Dutch Nick's were one and the same place...on top of all these absurdities I stated that this...murderer, after inflicting a wound upon himself that the reader ought to have seen would kill an elephant in the twinkling of an eye, jumped on his horse and rode four miles, waving his wife's reeking scalp in the air...

"My Bloody Massacre"

Dutch Nick's, or Empire City as it was later known, is a desert spot 4 miles east of Carson City near the Carson River, and south of U.S. Highway 50. Today, an industrial area surrounds the old Empire City graveyard where "Dutch Nick," Nick Ambrose is buried. It is dusty and full of sagebrush. The place has never known the shadow of a tree, never mind a whole pine forest. During the 1870's many large mining mills were located on the Carson River near Empire City.

Mark Twain did not appreciate the wrath heaped upon him by other papers. He angrily responded to their attacks. Twain called the writer of the *Bulletin's* attack, a "little person, oyster-brained idiot." But his defense could not hold back the wave of outrage. The *Bulletin* came back with:

POOR WRETCH, WE PITY HIM.—That unhappy mortal, the local of the Enterprise, *appears to be in a terrible agony at the castigation which he is receiving for the sin he committed in publishing that rascally hoax. Out of pity for the poor wretch's misery, we will not report upon him, and as a mark of the profundity of our pity for his sufferings, we advise him to depart in peace and sin no more. If he will drop that sin of well, we won't name it—"That doth so easily beset him," and leave off going to Chinatown, stop drinking whisky, pay his washerwoman, get up early, and not make a night hideous by howling his sorrows to the winds, he may yet become a partially decent member of society...*

October 30, 1863

Mark Twain, well aware of his own shortcomings, did not take these attacks well. They angered and eventually depressed him.

...Once more, in my self-complacent simplicity I felt that the time had arrived for me to rise up and be a reformer. I put this reformatory satire in the shape of a fearful "Massacre at Empire City." The San Francisco papers were making a great outcry about the iniquity of the Daney Silver-Mining Company, whose directors had declared a "cooked" or false dividend, for the purpose of increasing the value of their stock, so that they could sell out at a comfortable figure, and then scramble from under the tumbling concern. And while abusing the Daney, those papers did not forget to urge the public to get rid of their silver stocks and invest in sound and safe San Francisco stocks, such as the Spring Valley Water Company, etc. But right after this unfortunate juncture, behold the Spring Valley cooked a dividend too! And, so under the insidious mask of an invented "bloody massacre," I stole upon the public unawares with my scathing satire upon the dividend cooking system...

"My Bloody Massacre"

Editors and readers clamored for Mark Twain's head. Some subscribers canceled their subscriptions. Editors threatened they would never trust the *Enterprise* as long as Twain wrote for the paper.

Twain, wounded, offered to quit the paper. "Oh, Joe," he said, "I have ruined your business, and the only reparation I can make is to resign. You can never recover from this blow while I am on the paper."

"Nonsense," Joe Goodman countered. "We can furnish the people with news, but we can't supply them with sense...The flurry will pass. You must go ahead. We'll win out in the long run." And they did.

For as long as Mark Twain remained with the *Enterprise,* he was kidded about having murdered the Hopkins family. It was a running joke and he tired of it. But the "Massacre at Dutch Nick's" gave him notoriety and helped establish his reputation on the West Coast.

Years afterward, Dan De Quille wrote:

...Today not one man in a hundred in Nevada can remember anything written by Mark Twain while he was connected with the Enterprise, except this one item in regard to the shocking murder at Dutch Nick's; all else is forgotten, even by his oldest and most intimate friends.

Mark Twain's "Massacre at Dutch Nick's," may have failed at its intended purposes. But the furor over the "Massacre," dramatically taught Twain the power of the written word to excite and move people. Mark Twain was beginning to realize he possessed a powerful gift; writing was one of the ways he could communicate this gift to others.

4

One of the most important men Mark Twain met in Virginia City arrived just before Christmas, 1863. His real name was Charles F. Browne but he was known throughout America and Britain as Artemus Ward, a popular humorous writer and speaker. At twenty-eight, Ward was at the peak of his career. He had authored humorous books and articles; his articles and quips appeared regularly in newspapers and national magazines. He frequently lectured throughout America and Britain. Lecture isn't the right word; Ward's show was a stand-up comedy routine known as the "Babes in the Wood." Ward never mentioned the babes in the wood. He rambled for an hour or so about a wide range of topics. Ward's humor was based on ridiculous misspellings, mispronunciations, fumbled grammar, misuse of words, and garbled and incoherent sentences. Ward was brilliant but in his act he behaved like an uneducated idiot, making hilarious comments dead-pan, pretending in embarrassment not to understand why audiences roared. Ward was the common man's humorist, a sort of 1860's version of Rodney Dangerfield. Audiences loved him for his wit, warmth and humanity and Ward loved them back.

Beneath Ward's seeming naiveté and folksy

"Kettle-belly Browne" who looked after Artemus Ward, Twain and De Quille on their night of revelry in Virginia City.

style was a young man who cared and had important things to say. There was social criticism, satire of human weaknesses, pretentiousness and sentimentality. Ward was clever in the way Mark Twain was clever. When opera house owner Tom Maguire wired Ward and asked, "What will you take for forty nights in California?" Ward answered back, "Brandy and Water."

Ward's coming to the Comstock was like Marilyn Monroe visiting the troops. Excitement shot through the mining towns. The hardpressed miners were hungry for outside entertainment.

Ward was scheduled to speak twice in Virginia City at Maguire's Opera House and once in Gold Hill and Silver City. Watching Ward's shows Twain realized how he might better use his humor both to entertain and make money: it was on the stage like Ward. After all, he made people laugh; he could entertain; he could do what Ward did and he would try. With Ward's appearance, Mark Twain realized he too could earn a living on the stage as a speaker.

By the time Ward arrived in Virginia City, Mark Twain was familiar with Ward's work. Twain announced his coming in an article which imitated Ward's humorous writing:

...We understand that Artemus Ward contemplates visiting this region to deliver his lectures, and perhaps make some additions to his big "sho." In his last letter to us he appeared particularly anxious to "sekure a kupple ov horned todes; alsowe, a lizard which it may be persessed of 2 tales, or any komical snaix, an enny sich little unconsidered trifles, as the poets say, which they do not interest the kommun mind...Could you alsowe manage to gobbel up the skulp of the layte Missus Hopkins? I adore sich footprints of atrocity as it were, muchly. I was roominatin on gittin a bust of Mark Twain, but I've kwit kontemplatin the work. They tell me down heer too the Ba that the busts air so kommon it wood ony bee an waist of wax to git un kounterfit presentiment." We shall assist Mr. Ward in every possible way about making his Washoe collection and have no doubt but he will pick up many curious things during his sojourn,

The Golden Era, November 29, 1863

Artemus Ward arrived in Virginia City around December 23rd with his manager, E.E. Hingston. Mark Twain, Dan De Quille and Joe Goodman took Ward in like a brother. Ward made the *Enterprise* offices his home base and at times helped the boys get the paper out so they could get back to playing. Ward was only in Virginia City for a week but it was long enough for the four men to become friends; they were all Bohemians at heart. Mark Twain and Dan De Quille showed Ward the town. For a week they raised hell, got drunk, and carried on until dawn. In between parties Ward gave his lectures. Years later Dan De Quille recalled Ward's visit:

Virginia City was booming when Artemus Ward arrived to deliver his lecture. Comstockers received Artemus as a brother, and he seemed as much at home as if he had all his life been a resident of Virginia City. He remained on the Comstock several days, making the Enterprise *his headquarters. Mark Twain and I had the pleasure of showing him the town, and a real pleasure it was—a sort of circus, in fact—as he constantly overflowed with fun. He was anxious to get hold of the lingo and style of the miners, and we made him acquainted with several old forty-niners. The greetings among these men struck him as something new, and he began practicing, playing himself off as an old-timer...*

Artemus was full of curiosity about the Piute Indians and the Chinese. While he was here the Chinese had a pow-wow of some kind. A big tent was erected on a vacant lot in Chinatown, in which half a dozen yellow and purple-robed priests from San Francisco displayed their gods and received the vows of the faithful. One night Mark, Ward and I "took in" this and other Chinatown sights. We went to see Hop Sing, head of one company. Both insisted upon our testing various fiery drinks, such as rice "blandy" and other kinds of "blandy."

We narrowly escaped being caught in the midst of a fight that started between the rival companies, a fight in which about fifty shots were fired, killing one and wounding two or three.

In returning to the city from Chinatown we concluded to take a "near cut." Coming to a string of low frame houses, Artemus said the nearest cut was over the tops of the shanties, and crying "Follow your leader!" mounted a shed and the roof of a house. "Come ahead," cried he, "and we'll go up into town over the roofs of the houses. Follow your leader."

The "China blandy" was venturesome...soon we were all marching along over the roofs. We had not proceeded far before there came to our ears the command, "Halt there or I shoot," and we saw a man with a shotgun leveled at us. The man who had halted us was a watchman. He held his gun on us until we climbed down and marched up to him as ordered. Explanations followed and all was right as soon as our names were given.

"Right you are," said Artemus. "Take a few tickets and come to my show," and he poked over the fence to the man a handful of tickets.

"Thanks," said the watchman, and reaching behind into the tail of a long coat he drew forth a bottle that was almost as long as the barrel of his gun. "Good stuff," said he, as he poked the long bottle over the fence to us.

Mark and I feared to mix fighting American whiskey with warlike Chinese "blandy," but Artemus took the bottle, and as he placed it to his lips and elevated it toward the North Star it looked like a telescope. "Splendid," said he, as he lowered the instrument.

After this adventure we concluded to go to our rooms on B Street and all three turn into our big bed together, "three saints," as Artemus put it, "Mark, Luke and John." However, in going up Sutton Avenue there was heard "a sound of revelry by night." We were passing a huge barn of a building in which a couple of hurdy-gurdies were holding forth. Hurdies were something new to Ward, and he said he wanted to see the show.

On entering the dance hall Artemus announced our arrival by stating that we were "Babes in the Wood." As he was known by sight to most of those present there were at once "Cheers for Artemus Ward."

"Now," said Ward, "we three have got to have a dance together. It'll be a thing our offspring to the furthest generation will be proud of!"

So selecting three stalwart and capable girls as partners we danced to the unbound admiration of a large and enthusiastic audience headed by "Kettle-belly" Browne.

Artemus threw a twenty-dollar gold piece on the bar to pay for the dances and beer. The bartender took out about four times the usual rates and was raking Ward's double eagle into the till when "Kettle's" big hand came down upon the gold with a startling spat.

"No you don't!" said "Kettle,"—these gentlemen are friends of mine. This twenty don't go into the till until you hand out the right change!" Instantly the correct change was passed over to Ward.

Immediately the whole heart and soul of Artemus Ward went out to "Kettle." Said he to Browne: "We are three mere 'Babes in the Wood;' come along with us. We need you to take care of us."

So instead of going to bed we went forth under the guidance of the genial "Kettle." We went to hear the Cornish singers, and to see some of the big games, meeting with still further adventures in our wanderings, but everywhere fathered and guarded by the bulky, whole-souled and honest old Sonora miner, "Kettle-belly" Browne.

The first rays of the morning sun were gilding the peak of Mount Davidson. The "Babes" were out in front of Aaron Hooper's saloon—where happened to be some convenient packing cases—for a mouthful of fresh air...

San Francisco *Examiner*, March 19, 1893

Mark Twain, Dan De Quille and Joe Goodman attended each of Ward's performances. Twain carefully studied Ward's act and noted the techniques Ward used to work his audience. Twain would later employ some of these in his own lectures. Commenting on Ward's "Babes in the Wood" Twain wrote,

There are perhaps fifty subjects treated in it, and there is a passable point in every one of them, and a healthy laugh, also, for any of God's creatures...The man who is capable of listening to the 'Babes in the Wood' from beginning to end without laughing either inwardly of outwardly must have done murder, or at least meditated on it, at some time during his life.

Virginia *Evening Bulletin*, December 28, 1863

During his visit, Ward and Twain spoke of their careers. Ward saw Twain as an emerging talent. He encouraged him to seek an Eastern audience for his writings and offered to write on Twain's behalf a "powerfully convincing note" of introduction to the editor of the New York *Mercury*. Less than two months later, Mark Twain's first Eastern article, "For Sale or to Rent," was published in the *Mercury*, February 7, 1864, followed two weeks later by "Those Blasted Children." The publication of these articles was likely due to Ward's intervention on Twain's behalf. These articles and the publication of "Jim Smiley and His Jumping Frog" in the New York *Saturday Press* in 1865 helped Mark Twain make his reputation in the East.

Perhaps the most important thing Ward did for Twain was to rekindle Twain's desire to perform on the stage. Twain had toyed with the idea of becoming an actor but had not pursued it. Twain loved talking and story telling; he was good at it and he enjoyed having a crowd's undivided attention. After seeing Ward perform on the stage, Mark Twain realized this was something he could do and make money at.

Less than a month later Mark Twain gave his first lecture at Carson City, a benefit for the First Presbyterian Church for which his brother Orion was an elder. Mark Twain's lecture attracted a larger audience than Ward. The room was packed; at a dollar a head, Twain raised more than $200 for the church. This lecture was the beginning of a highly successful speaking career which lasted the rest of Twain's life.

6

Mark Twain seems to have entered an important transition period between November, 1863 and the end of February, 1864. During these four months, Mark Twain transformed himself from a prankster journalist to a serious committed writer. His writing improved in content and style. His reputation as a humorist and journalist grew; he began to win the respect of peers and readers. His writing began to make a genuine impact on the Nevada community. Most importantly, Twain himself began to realize that his writing could affect his world.

Twain spent most of this transition period in Carson City as a political reporter for the *Enterprise*. He arrived in Carson City November 2 to report the Constitutional Convention. He made a brief trip back to Virginia City in early December but was again in Carson for the close of the Convention December 11. Exhausted from the whirl of day and night politics, December 12 he left for Lake Tahoe by himself for a rest. Twain returned to Virginia City for Artemus Ward's arrival December 23. He left for Carson City shortly after New Year's, 1864. January 12 to February 20, 1864 he reported the third Territorial Legislature in Carson City.

During this four month transition period, there were a number of positive influences on Twain's thinking and writing.

Fellow *Enterprise* journalists had definitely influenced Mark Twain's writing development during the thirteen months he had reported for the *Enterprise*. Editor Joe Goodman taught Twain to stick to the facts and Twain had largely followed Goodman's advice. There were the bursts of fiction, the "Petrified Man," and the "Massacre At Dutch Nick's" but these had only increased his reputation as a humorist and regional celebrity. Co-editor Rollin Daggett had taught Twain to speak his mind and attack injustice. Jim Townsend, a marvelous story teller, whose humor and style was akin to Twain's, had shared many stories with Twain during long bull sessions. These stories and Townsend's style would work there way into Twain's writing. Dan De Quille had recently returned to Virginia City; he and Twain became roommates. De Quille was a positive example of a hard working journalist who took his work seriously and strove for accuracy. Dan encouraged Mark in his writing and often made helpful suggestions which tempered Twain's radical views. Most importantly, the *Enterprise* staff was a constant source of friendship and support. Twain felt accepted as a person and writer.

Twain's increased writing output during this period helped Twain to improve his writing. He wrote a 4,000 word political dispatch five days a week. On Sunday he wrote a long personalized summary of political and social doings. Mark Twain each day wrote the equivalent of ten, typed, doubled-spaced pages, six days a week, sixty pages a week! Twain wrote enough in one month to fill two books. Those who considered Twain lazy, may not have realized the time and energy good writing re-

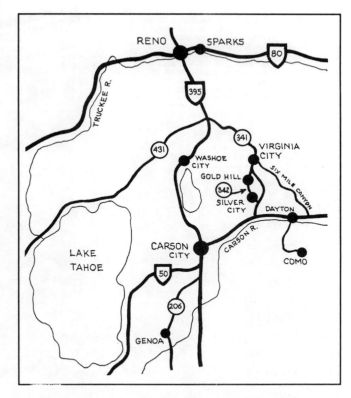

quires. Anyone who has struggled with a twenty page term paper learns this. To add to the difficulties, the invention of the typewriter was years away. Everything had to be written by hand in pencil or by quill and ink. If a writer made a mistake or wished to change a sentence, he either crossed it out and made a mess or rewrote the entire article by hand. It was a grind that required time, labor and commitment.

Another important factor was Mark Twain's change in attitude towards his work. Where in the past he had collected or invented news simply to fill his columns, now Twain was taking his writing more seriously. As political reporter for the most powerful newspaper in the Territory, Twain understood his responsibilities as a journalist. His articles were now mostly concerned with issues which affected the community and the Territory. Twain was concerned about the burgeoning State. There were laws he wanted passed, bills he opposed and he expressed deep feelings in his articles about them. His humor and satire were still there, but his articles were far more serious. He seemed to have a new confidence in his ideas

The Third House, a group of young men who gathered after legislative sessions and lampooned politicians. Mark Twain is second from the left with his arm up and appearing to be holding a pipe. Sandy Baldwin is the small man front row, third from right.

and he worked hard to win people to his thinking.

This change in attitude may have partially been caused by Mark Twain's growing older. November 30 he turned twenty-eight. Practical minded, Mark Twain must have realized time was passing. Youth would not last forever. Twain appears to have finally committed himself to writing as a career. His heightened regional success, Artemus Ward's visit, encouragement, and inspiration had certainly helped Twain make up his mind.

Other important influences on his writing

and thinking during this period were the intelligent, educated and aggressive men with whom Twain daily and often nightly interacted. Most were attorneys, skilled with words in writing and speaking. Living and working among the best men in Nevada Territory for the greater part of four months no doubt stimulated Mark Twain.

Among these men was Alexander "Sandy" Baldwin. At twenty-two, Baldwin was one of the leading attorneys in Nevada Territory. Baldwin was brilliant; at fourteen he entered the University of Virginia; at nineteen he was a district attorney in California. As a Virginia City attorney, Baldwin quickly earned more than a half million dollars representing mining companies in litigation. He was short, cocky, and often brilliant. Bill Stewart was often Baldwin's adversary in court. During one courtroom battle, Baldwin kept interrupting

Theodore Winters, who along with Sandy Baldwin, presented Mark Twain with a gold watch. Winters' house still stands along U.S. Highway 395 in Washoe City.

Stewart. Finally Stewart yelled at Baldwin, "You little shrimp, if you interrupt me again, I'll eat you."

Baldwin came back with, "If you do, you'll have more brains in your belly than you've ever had in your head."

Baldwin was later a U.S. District Court Judge in Nevada Territory.

It was Sandy Baldwin along with Theodore Winters who presented Mark Twain with a $200 gold watch upon Twain's election as President of the Third House, a group of reporters, legislator and citizens who gathered in saloons to ridicule legislative proceedings.

William "Bill " Stewart was the most prominent lawyer in Nevada. He was tall, intelligent, witty and a cunning courtroom strategist. Stewart made a fortune representing Virginia City

mining companies and owned the finest house in Carson City.

Born in New York, raised in Ohio, Stewart attended Yale before coming to California in 1850. He became a prospector, studied law and was admitted to the California bar in 1852. In 1854 he was attorney general of California. In 1860 Stewart moved to Nevada, served as a member of the Territorial Council in 1861 and the 1863 Constitutional Convention where Stewart lobbied against taxation of mining properties.

Bill Stewart and Governor James Nye became the first Nevadans elected to the Senate in 1864. Stewart served two long terms: 1864-75 and 1887-1905.

Three years after Twain had left Virginia City, he showed up at Bill Stewart's home in Washington, D.C. Twain told Stewart he was writing a book, *The Innocents Abroad,* and needed a temporary job. Stewart hired Twain as his personal secretary and let him stay at his home in Washington.

William "Billy" Claggett was a boyhood friend of Sam Clemens. Clemens had met Claggett in Keokuk, Iowa while Sam was working for one of Orion's newspapers. Claggett was then studying law.

Clemens and Claggett were reunited in Carson City in the winter of 1861-62. Claggett traveled with Clemens to Unionville that winter. Claggett remained at Unionville where he opened a law practice. There he was elected to the Legislature in 1862 and to the House of Representatives in 1864. Claggett was known for his great oratorical skill and his mop of unruly hair.

Jack Simmons was Speaker of the House during the second Territorial Legislature. He was a close friend of Mark Twain's and a leading member of the Third House.

Abraham Curry was the principal founder of Carson City. Curry came to Nevada Territory in 1858 and had prospected in Gold Canyon. He was one of the discoverers of the Gould and Curry mine, one of the richest Virginia City

Hank Monk, the notorious stage driver who told Horace Greeley, "Keep your seat Horace, and I'll get you there on time," and Hank did. The story is told in Chapter 20 of *Roughing It*. Monk was Mark Twain's friend.

mines. Curry sold his share for a small sum and settled in Carson City where he built the Warm Springs Hotel. "Old Abe" Curry served as a representative to the second Territorial Legislature and councilman to the third. He was a good friend of Twain's. Twain praised Curry's many community contributions in *Roughing It*.

Tom Fitch and his wife lived across the hall from Mark Twain and Dan De Quille. Fitch was editor of the Virginia *Daily Union* and later started the short lived, *Occidental* in March, 1864. Fitch was a journalist, lawyer and a politician noted for his oratory and dubbed by his friends the "Silver Tongued."

Born in New York, Fitch migrated to California where he worked for newspapers in San Francisco and Placerville. Later admitted to the California bar, Fitch was elected to the Califor-

nia Legislature in 1862. Fitch came to Nevada in 1863 and was Storey County delegate to the Constitutional Convention in 1863; he served as Washoe City district attorney 1865-66 and in 1868 was elected to Congress.

James Nye was the first Territorial Governor of Nevada, 1861-64, and elected United States Senator from Nevada in 1864; he served eight years. A rascally politician and clever in his dealings with people, Nye was first a district attorney and judge in Madison County, New York, and afterward president of the Metropolitan Board of Police in New York City.

As Governor of Nevada Territory, James Nye was boss to Orion Clemens. As the leading politicians, Nye and Orion Clemens were important socially. There were many get togethers at Nye's residence; Mark Twain, Orion and Mollie Clemens and other legislators were regular attendants. Mark Twain admired Nye's political skill and his sense of humor. Though Nye was years older, Twain and Nye were good friends. Mark Twain's first speech was in part a satire of Governor Nye. Governor Nye accepted the humor in stride and later bestowed on Twain one of the coveted notarial commissions. As notary public, Twain earned extra money. Twain gave much space to Governor Nye in *Roughing It*.

Theodore Winters was a successful Washoe Valley rancher and farmer. He was a large stock holder in the Ophir Mining Company, owned celebrated race horses and maintained a race track at his Washoe City ranch. Winters was involved in Territorial politics and was a member of the Third House. Winters paid half of the $200 for the gold watch he and Sandy Baldwin presented to Mark Twain upon his election as President of the Third House. Theodore Winters' home, where Mark Twain often visited, still stands in Washoe City along the east side of U.S. Highway 395 between Carson City and the Virginia City turnoff.

Hal Clayton was the presiding officer of the Third House during the first and second Territorial legislatures. In 1860 he was the prosecuting attorney in Carson City. Like Clemens, Clayton was a southerner; unlike Clemens, Clayton spoke out passionately for the Confederacy. Clayton was arrested by Union soldiers July, 1863 for "persisting in the utterance of disloyal sentiments." Clayton was later released and again supervised Third House proceedings during the 1864, 1867 and 1869 legislative sessions.

Mark Twain frequently mentioned these and other men in his Carson City reports. They were often the butts of his humor. Their willingness to accept public embarrassment in good humor is evidence of their friendship and their high regard for Twain.

Twain carefully selected the men with whom he interacted. He preferred educated, successful men with sharp minds who knew how to enjoy themselves. He had a weakness for attorneys and preachers. Both professions employed good talkers and men who possessed a deep commitment to justice. Twain had considered both professions himself. But he had no patience for the legal mumbo-jumbo the law profession required and he never considered himself religious enough to become a preacher though he enjoyed preaching all sorts of messages throughout his life.

It is surprising Mark Twain chose to associate with such men. All were college educated. Mark Twain was self-conscious about his lack of formal education. On the other hand, having traveled widely for ten years and worked as a printer, river boat pilot and prospector, Mark Twain had met all sorts of people, seen many sides of life and experienced the wide open, real world at its fullest. What he lacked in formal education, Twain had made up in experience. Still, there were moments he felt ill at ease because of his lack of education. But you would not have suspected so. Twain not only acted as an equal to these men, he often outshone them by his wit and attention getting behavior.

November 2 the Constitutional Convention convened in Carson City. Mark Twain now

entered his most influential period as journalist for the *Territorial Enterprise*. While living in Carson City, Twain stayed with his brother Orion, sister-in-law, Mollie, and his niece, Jennie.

The Convention lasted 32 days. Mark Twain attended each session, made pencil notes in his notebook and afterward wrote a summary of the daily proceedings. Twain was aided by A.J. Marsh, a shorthand expert whom the *Enterprise* had borrowed from the Sacramento *Union*. Though political debates and the dull hours of haggling often bored Twain, he liked the excitement of back room politicking and enjoyed being in the thick of activity. He enjoyed the camaraderie of his old friends Billy Claggett and Jack Simmons. There was a good deal of joking during legislative meetings. January 15, 1864, "the Chair announced Mr. Sam. L. Clemens as entitled to a seat as Reporter for the House, while the courtesy of that body should continue to hold out." Several days later Twain reported, "I am here...on my good behavior, as it were..." Legislators treated Twain as if he were a member of the House rather than a reporter. After legislative sessions members of the Third House gathered in various Carson saloons. A favorite haunt was the Corner Bar at the Ormsby House, Carson's only substantial hotel.

Mark Twain wrote daily dispatches and weekly summaries. The daily reports were dry news items published without a by-line or signed "Sam Clemens." The weekly reports written on Sunday were casual and humorous. These gave news about legislative doings, personal comments on the activities of legislators and local events; the Sunday summaries were signed, "Mark Twain." In his autobiography Mark Twain said, "Every Sunday I wrote a letter to the paper [from Carson City] in which I made a resume of the week's legislative work, and in order that it might be readable I put no end of seasoning into it. I signed these letters 'Mark Twain.' " Twain believed it was important to entertain readers as well as inform.

Twain freely gossiped about local characters. Twain understood that people liked reading about other people. He explained this to his sister Pamela in a letter:

Pamela, you wouldn't do for a local reporter— because you don't appreciate the interest that attaches to names. *An item is of no use unless it speaks of some* person, *& not then, unless that person's* name *is distinctly mentioned. The most interesting one can write to an absent friend, is one that treats of* persons *he has been acquainted with rather than the public events of the day. Now you speak of a young lady who wrote to Hallie Benson that she had seen me, & you didn't mention her* name. *It was just a mere chance that I ever guessed who she was—but I did finally, though I don't remember her name, now.*

March 18, 1864 to Pamela Moffett

Mark Twain mentioned a total of more than 250 people in his daily dispatches.

Nothing disturbed Mark Twain more than pretentious wind-bags. Attending the Constitutional Convention, was a long-winded delegate from Aurora, L.O. Sterns, whom Twain had likely met while in Aurora. Toward the end of the Constitutional Convention, Twain made fun of Sterns' wandering speeches:

Mr. Sterns said—Mr. President, I am opposed, I am hostile, I am uncompromisingly against this proposition to tax the mines. I will go further, sir. I will openly assert sir, that I am not in favor of this proposition. It is wrong—entirely wrong...we owe it to our constituents to defeat this pernicious measure. Incorporate it into your constitution, sir,...the gaunt forms of want, poverty, and starvation, and despair will shortly walk in the high places of this once happy and beautiful land. Add it to your fundamental law, sir, and (as we stated yesterday by the gentleman from Lander) God will cease to smile upon your labors. In the language (of my colleague), I entreat you, sir, and gentlemen, inflict not this mighty iniquity upon generations yet unborn! Heed the prayers of the people and be merciful! Ah, sir, the quality of mercy is not strained, so to speak (as has been appropriately suggested heretofore,) but droppeth like the gentle dew from Heaven, as it were. The gentleman from Douglas has said this law would be unconstitutional, and I cordially agree with him. Therefore, let its course to the ramparts be hurried—let the flames that shook the battle's wreck, shine round it o'er the dead—let it go hence to that undiscovered country from whose bourne no traveler returns (as hath been remarked by the gentleman from Washoe, Mr. Shamp,) and in this guarding and protecting the poor miner, let us endeavor to do unto others as we would that others should do unto us (as was very justly and properly observed by Jesus Christ upon a former occasion.)

The one troubling feature of the newly created state Constitution, was a clause which provided for the taxation of mining properties. Mark Twain opposed the measure and feared voters would reject the Constitution because of it. Bill Stewart went back and forth on mining taxation. Twain finally took him to task:

...Bill Stewart is always construing something— eternally distorting facts and principles. He would climb out of his coffin and construe the burial service. He is a long-legged, bull headed, whopper-jawed, constructionary monomaniac. Give him a chance to construe the sacred law, and there wouldn't be a damned soul in perdition in a month...He construed the constitution, last night...He gave the public to understand that the clause providing for the taxation of the mines meant nothing in particular; that he wanted the privilege of construing that section to suit himself, that a mere hole in the ground was not a mine, and it wasn't property (he slung that in because he has a costly well on his premises in Virginia;) and that it would be a difficult matter to determine in our courts what does really constitute a mine. Do you see his drift? Well, I do. He will prove to the satisfaction of the courts that there are only two definite kinds of mine; that one of these is an excavation from which metallic ores or other mineral substances are "DUG"...Then of course, the miners will know enough to stop "digging" and go

to blasting. Bill Stewart will then show, easily enough, that these fellows claims are not "mines" according to the dictionary, and consequently cannot be taxed. He will show that the only other species of "mine" is a "pronominal adjective," and proceed to prove that there is nothing in the Constitution that will permit the state to tax the English grammar. He will demonstrate that a mere hole in the ground is not a mine, and is not liable to taxation. The end will be that a year from now we shall all own in these holes in the ground, but no man will acknowledge that he owns in a "mine"; and about that time custom, and policy, and construction, combined will have taught us to speak of the staunch old bulwark of the State as, "The Great Gould & Curry Hole-in-the-Ground"...

Twain's criticism of Stewart may seem exaggerated, but it would not have been unlike Stewart to use this argument to exempt mines from taxation.

When the Constitution was finally completed, Twain gave his opinion:

...It was an excellent piece of work in some respects, but it had one or two unfortunate defects which debarred it from assuming to be an immaculate conception. The chief of these was a clause authorizing the taxing of the mines. The people will not stand that. There are some 30,000 gold and silver mining incorporations here, or mines, or claims, or which you please, or all, if it suits you better. Very little of the kind of property thus represented is improved yet, or "developed" as we call it...And until it does begin to pay dividends, the people will not consent that it shall be burdened and hindered by taxation. Therefore, I am satisfied they will refuse to ratify our new constitution on the 19th...

Enterprise, January 4, 1864

Twain was right. Voters rejected the state Constitution five to one.

Then there was the business of the Great Seal of the State. Twain wrote:

...It had snow-capped mountains in it; and tun-

nels, and shafts, and pickaxes, and quartz-mills, and pack-trains, and mule-teams. These things were good; what there were of them. And it has railroads in it, and telegraphs, and stars, and suspension bridges, and other romantic fictions foreign to sand and sage-brush. But the richest of it was the motto. It took them thirty days to decide whether it should be "Volens et Potens" (which they said meant "Able and Willing")...We have an animal here whose surname is the "jackass rabbit." It is three feet long, has legs like a counting-house stool, ears of monstrous length, and no tail to speak of. It is swifter than a greyhound, and as meek and harmless as an infant. I might mention, also, that it is as handsome as most infants...Well, somebody proposed as a substitute for that pictorial Great Seal, a figure of a jackass-rabbit reposing in the shade of his native sage-brush, with the motto "Volens enough, but not so d——d Potens,"...

Enterprise, January 4, 1864

Following the Constitutional Convention, the State Nominating Convention met and candidates for various political offices were chosen. Of these political candidates Twain wrote:

..they all owe me something for traducing and vilifying them in the public prints, and thus exciting sympathy for them on the score of persecution, and securing their nomination...I elected those fellows, and I shall take care that I am fairly remunerated for it...

The most striking aspect of Twain's articles during this time, is his concern for issues which affected the community. In "A Gorgeous Swindle" he attacked a fraudulent investment company which had swindled "multitudes of the poorest classes." He attacked Bill Stewart for supporting a clause which would have permitted taxation of undeveloped mining properties. Following the death of Orion's daughter, Jennie, February 1, Twain lashed out at the sole Carson undertaker who pilfered the pockets of citizens at a time of terrible sorrow. Twain wrote of this parasite:

There is a system of extortion going on here which is absolutely terrific, and I wonder if the Carson Independent has never ventilated the subject. There seems to be only one undertaker in the town, and he owns the only graveyard in which it is at all high-toned or aristocratic to be buried. Consequently, when a man loses his wife or his child, or his mother, this undertaker makes him sweat for it. I appeal to those whose firesides death has made desolate during the few fatal weeks just past, if I am not speaking the truth. Does not this undertaker take advantage of that unfortunate delicacy which prevents a man from disputing an unjust bill for services rendered in burying the dead, to extort ten-fold more than his labors are worth? ...This undertaker charges a hundred and fifty for a pine coffin that cost him twenty or thirty, and fifty dollars for a grave that did not cost him ten—and this at a time when his ghastly services are required at least seven times a week...What Carson needs is a few more undertakers—there is vacant land enough here for a thousand cemeteries.

The editor of the Carson *Independent* wrote an editorial response to Twain's article. He denied knowing about the undertaker's extortion and wrote that it was the duty of citizens to, "ventilate the matter. We have heard no complaints."

Mark Twain was furious. He lashed out at the incompetent editor:

Having had no use for a coffin himself, the editor "therefore knows nothing about the price of such things." It is my unsolicited opinion that he knows very little about anything. And anybody who will read his paper calmly and dispassionately for a week will endorse that opinion. And more especially his knowing nothing about Carson, is not surprising; he seldom mentions that town in his paper. If the Second Advent were to occur here, you would hear of it first in some other newspaper. He says, "If any of our citizens think they have been imposed upon in this particular, it is their duty to ventilate the matter." ...Where did you get your notion of the duties of a journalist from? Any editor in the world will say it is your duty to ferret out these abuses, and your duty to correct them. What are you paid for?

What use are you to the community? What are you fit for as conductor of a newspaper, if you cannot do these things. Are you paid to know nothing, and keep on writing about it every day? How long do you suppose such a jack-legged newspaper as yours would be supported or tolerated in Carson, if you had a rival no larger than a foolscap sheet, but with something in it, and whose editor would know, or at least have energy enough to find out, whether a neighboring paper abused one of the citizens justly or unjustly? That paragraph which I have copied, seems to mean one thing, while in reality it means another. Its true translation is, for instance: "Our name is Independent—*that is, in different phrase,* Opinionless. *We have no opinions on any subject— we reside permanently on the fence. In order to have no opinions, it is necessary that we should know nothing—therefore, if this undertaker is fleecing the people, we will not know it, and then we shall not offend him. We have heard no complaints and we shall make no inquiries, lest we do hear some,"...*

Mr. Curry [Abe Curry] says if the people will come forward and take hold of the matter, a city cemetery can be prepared and fenced in a week, and at a trivial cost—a cemetery from which a man can set out for Paradise or perdition just as respectably as he can from the undertaker's private grounds at present...

Enterprise, February 13, 1864

There were bills and laws Mark Twain lobbied for and against. He was against a telegraph bill which virtually gave one company a monopoly. When another "pet" bill was laid to rest by legislators, Twain took them aside one night:

While I was absent a moment, yesterday, on important business, taking a drink, the House, with its accustomed engaging unanimity, knocked one of my pet bills higher than a kite, without a dissenting voice. I convened the members in extra session last night, and deluged them with blasphemy, after which I entered into a solemn compact with them, whereby, in consideration of their re-instating my bill, I was to make an ample apology for all the mean things I

had said about them for passing that infamous, unchristian, infernal telegraph bill the other day. I also promised to apologize for all the mean things that the other people had published against them for their depraved action aforesaid. They re-instated my pet to-day...I hereby solemnly apologize for their rascally conduct in passing the infamous telegraph bill above mentioned. Under ordinary circumstances, they never would have done such a thing—but upon that occasion I think they had been fraternizing with Claggett and Simmons at the White House, and were under the vicious influence of Humboldt whiskey. Consequently, they were not responsible...to anybody on earth or in heaven.—Mark Twain
Enterprise, February 12, 1864

Twain called the telegraph bill a "monstrosity" and as late as April, he was complaining about its effects:

...The infernal telegraph monopoly saddled upon this Territory by the last Legislature, in the passage of that infamous special Humboldt telegraph bill...is bearing its fruits, and the people here, as well as at Virginia, are beginning to wince under illegal and exorbitant telegraphic charges...The moment that law received the Governor's signature last winter, you will recollect the Telegraph Company doubled their prices for dispatches to and from San Francisco. And that is not the worst they have done, if common report be true. This common report says the telegraph is used by its owners to aid them in stock-gambling schemes. I recollect on the night the jury went out in the Savage and North Potosi case and failed to agree, our San Francisco dispatch failed to come to hand and the reason assigned was that a dispatch of 3,000 words was being sent from Virginia to San Francisco and the line could not be used for other messages. Now that Telegraph Company may have made money by trading in North Potosi on that occasion, but who is young enough to believe they ever got two dollars and a half for that voluminous imaginary dispatch? That telegraph is a humbug...
Virginia Evening Bulletin, April 28, 1864

Because of Twain's moral stance in his articles, fellow reporters and writers dubbed Twain the Moral Phenomenon and the name stuck. Beyond the humor, fellow reporters and readers were recognizing that Mark Twain was no ordinary just lay-out-the-facts reporter. This was a man with deep moral convictions who would not let fools and swindlers escape without giving them a sound thrashing. Not if Twain could help it.

Much of Mark Twain's humor is derived from his self-mockery; he pokes fun at his laziness, calls himself a fool and a liar but resigns himself; for all the good and bad, he is what he is.

One example of this behavior is an episode which took place in Virginia City. *Enterprise* jokers were forever playing practical jokes on Twain hoping he would explode in a rage of epithets and profanity. These were shows not to be missed. One of their favorite stunts was stealing the candle Twain used in the evenings to write by.

On one such occasion when Twain had again found his candle missing, a passing minister, Mr. Rising, happened to walk in and caught Twain cursing the thieves who had hidden his candle. Finally, Twain turned to Rising.

"I know, Mr. Rising, I know it's wicked to talk like this; I know it is wrong. I know I shall certainly go to hell for it. But if you had a candle, Mr. Rising, and those thieves should carry it off every night, I know that you would say, just as I say, Mr. Rising, *God damn their impenitent souls, may they roast in hell for a million years!*"

"Maybe I should, Mr. Clemens, but I should try to say, 'Forgive them, Father, they know not what they do.'"

"Oh, well! If you put it on the ground that they are just fools, that alters the case, as I am one of that class myself. Come in and we'll try to forgive them and forget about it."

Mark Twain's self-mockery and his frankness about his shortcomings endears him to readers. He understood there is good and bad in each of us and try as hard as we might, most of us fall short of being as virtuous as we would like to be. Thank God the Almighty loves us in spite of ourselves.

6

A number of circumstances eventually led Twain to leave Virginia City at the end of May, 1864. For the most part, he was simply fed up with the isolated mining town and tired of living in one place for so long. In a letter to his brother a few days before leaving Virginia City, Twain wrote, "...Washoe [Nevada Territory] has long since grown irksome to us, & we [Steve Gillis, an *Enterprise* printer and Twain's friend] want to leave it... " [Letter to Orion Clemens, May 26, 1864]

Besides it was spring, and it seemed with spring Twain got the urge to travel. Twain wrote of leaving Virginia City,

I began to get tired of staying in one place so long. There was no longer satisfying variety in going down to Carson [City] to report the proceedings of the legislature once a year, and horse races and pumpkin shows once in three months...I wanted to see San Francisco. I wanted to go somewhere. I wanted—I did not know what I wanted. I had the "spring fever" and wanted a change, principally, no doubt.

Chapter 55 *Roughing It*

And something else had happened. After drinking one evening, Twain and De Quille went down to the *Enterprise* offices. There while drunk Twain wrote a scathing article about a group of Carson City ladies whom he mistakenly believed had misappropriated donations from the Sanitary Fund, a charity which helped wounded soldiers. Twain never intended the article to be published. But he mistakenly left it on the printer's table, and the printer, believing it was meant for publication, put it in the next day's paper.

The Carson ladies were furious when the article appeared. They demanded to know who the author was and asked for an apology. Twain was sorry the article had been published; he apologized publicly and privately. Still, the ruckus got so bad, one woman's husband went hunting for Twain with a gun.

In addition, Twain, who had become editor in Joe Goodman's absence, wrote a series of editorials in which he accused James Laird, editor of a rival paper, of his ungenerous support of the Sanitary Fund. Twain and Laird spit a series of heated letters back and forth in their papers. Hostilities reached a pitch when Twain called Laird, "an unmitigated liar," and challenged Laird to a duel. Dueling and challenges to duel were against Nevada law. A friend suggested it was in Twain's best interest to leave Virginia City until the dust settled.

For these reasons, on May 29, 1864, Mark Twain boarded the stage for San Francisco with Steve Gillis and Joe Goodman. Twain wrote of leaving Virginia City:

It was not without regret that I took a last look at the tiny flag (it was thirty-five feet long and ten feet wide) fluttering like a lady's handkerchief from the top most peak of Mt. Davidson, two thousand feet above Virginia's roofs, and felt that doubtless I was bidding a permanent farewell to a city which had afforded me the most vigorous enjoyment of my life I had ever experienced.

Chapter 55 *Roughing It*

Though at the time he said he would never return to Virginia City, he returned twice, after he had earned greater notoriety in San Francisco. [For more on Mark Twain in Virginia City, read the author's, *Mark Twain: His Life In Virginia City, Nevada.*]

Virginia City and the Comstock Lode

The great "Comstock lode" stretched its opulent length straight through the town from north to south, and every mine on it was in diligent process of development. One of these mines employed six hundred and seventy-five men, and in the matter of elections the adage was, "as the 'Gould and Curry' goes, so goes the city."

Chapter 43 *Roughing It*

Sam Clemens arrived in Virginia City in September, 1862. He worked as a reporter for the *Territorial Enterprise*, then the leading newspaper on the West Coast. On January 31, 1863, Clemens first signed "Mark Twain," to a dispatch from Carson City. The pseudonym had little to do with Clemens' Mississippi River days, but much to do with his drinking in Virginia City. Mark Twain left Virginia City in late May, 1864. He returned to Virginia City twice, in 1866 and 1868, where he lectured at Piper's Opera House.

The Comstock Lode mining district is located in the Washoe Mountains about 15 miles northeast of Carson City. It can be reached from Reno by taking U.S. Highway 395, 8 miles south to Nevada Highway 341 and 12 miles up steep Geiger Grade to Virginia City.

Virginia City can be reached from Carson City by taking U.S. Highway 50, 8 miles east to the Virginia City turnoff. Then take Nevada Highway 342, 7 miles up Gold Canyon to Virginia City. RV's, campers and trucks with travel trailers should use the truck route, Nevada Highway 341, which splits off from Highway 342, just this side, or east of Silver City.

The Comstock Lode mining district was comprised of several communities which sprang up in or near Gold Canyon: Johntown, Silver City, Gold Hill, Virginia City and American Flat. Nevada Highway 342, reached via Highway 50, climbs up a portion of Gold Canyon.

As you head up Gold Canyon from Carson City on Nevada Highway 342, Silver City is the first community you come to. Two miles beyond is what remains of Gold Hill. A half mile

farther and over the Divide is Virginia City, built on the east face of Mt. Davidson (formerly Sun Mountain.) American Flat, is west and over the hill from Gold Hill.

Just south of Silver City, a dirt road heads south down Gold Canyon near the truck route turn-off. The Johntown site, the very first settlement in the area, is located one mile down Gold Canyon. Nothing remains of this historic settlement.

In the spring of 1850, a Mormon emigrant party camped beside the Carson River near what is now Dayton. They were on the emigrant road from Utah west across Nevada to California. The road happened to pass through the sandy flats between the Washoe and Pine Nut mountains along the Carson River. They intended to reach Placerville but on learning the Sierra passes were still snowed in, they decided to camp under the cottonwoods beside the river until the passes cleared.

The Mormons were camped near the mouth of Gold Canyon. With little to do, some men ventured up the Canyon and began panning for gold. They discovered enough gold dust to pay for beans and bacon but not enough to make them stay and work the site. With visions of greater fortunes awaiting them in the California gold fields, the Mormon party moved on and left their discovery.

Not long afterward, Spofford Hall built a log house at what is now Dayton near the mouth of Gold Canyon. This was the first permanent settlement in the region and was known as Hall's Station, later McMartin's Station. Here weary emigrants bought or traded for needed supplies.

Word of the Gold Canyon placer discovery was passed on to others. By the spring of 1852, a considerable number were working the lower portion of the Canyon and making $5 to $10 a day in their rockers. The following spring, their number increased to 200-300. During the spring run-off there was enough water in the Canyon to placer mine. But in summer the seasonal streams dried up and there was little or no

Looking down from Mt. Davidson to Virginia City. The large piles of white sand are the tailings from the major mines. Photo was taken in the late 1870's.

water. Only fifty or so miners stayed through the summer to work the Canyon.

As the lower Canyon was worked out, miners pushed farther up. The hamlet of Johntown was built a few miles up from Hall's Station, a sorry collection of dugouts and log buildings. From 1856-58 Johntown was the center of mining activity. Here miners gathered after work at "Dutch Nick's", Nick Ambrose's store, where a horrible form of whisky was sold called "tarantula juice"— strong enough to kill rattle snakes or spiders if a man was bitten, or so the miners bragged. Ambrose supplied the miners with room and board, that is, food and a blanket for about $10-14 a week. A miner found the nearest clump of sagebrush and curled up with his blanket underneath the stars. "Dutch Nick" would later find his way into one of Mark Twain's most well known hoaxes, the "Massacre At Dutch Nick's."

In 1852, Edgar Allen and Hosea B. Grosch, brothers, built a stone cabin about one mile above Johntown near Silver City. The Grosch brothers had considerable knowledge of mining and metallurgy. They brought with them a collection of scientific books, furnaces for smelting and testing, and chemicals and equipment for assaying. The brothers kept to themselves and spoke little of their mining activities. It was later learned the Grosches had discovered rich deposits of silver ore near Mt. Davidson. It was the first such discovery in the area.

But in 1857, Hosea while mining, severely injured his foot with a pick-axe. The wound became infected and Hosea died within several days. Allen, in his grief, left the area and attempted to cross the Sierra in the winter. Both feet froze and had to be amputated. Allen died from the shock of the operation. With the Grosch brothers died the whereabouts of the rich silver ore deposits.

In January, 1859, there was a spell of good weather. The Johntowners spread out and began prospecting. Saturday, January 28, 1859, Henry "Old Pancake" Comstock, John Bishop, James "Old Virginia" Finney and others discovered placer gold at the head of Gold Canyon where Gold Hill is located today, about one mile south of Virginia City. The men claimed the diggings for placer mining. They did not know that beneath them was one of the richest bodies of silver and gold ore in the world. The miners now made $15-20 a day working the Gold Hill surface diggings. The rest of the Johntowners eventually moved up to Gold Hill. Nick Ambrose followed his clientele. Gold Hill later became the sight of some of the richest Comstock mines: the Belcher, Crown Point, Yellow Jacket, Imperial and Kentuck.

Six Mile Canyon, about a mile north of Gold Canyon, runs parallel to Gold Canyon and leads down from Mt. Davidson to the flats near the Carson River. Gold had also been discovered in Six Mile Canyon and miners had gradually worked their way up the Canyon to the foot of Mt. Davidson. Two of these were Irish placer miners, Peter O'Riley and Pat McLaughlin.

June 1, 1859, O'Riley and McLaughlin were working at the head of Six Mile Canyon at what is today called the Ophir Pit, at the north end of Virginia City above A Street. O'Riley and McLaughlin were making a paltry $1.50-2.00 a day. They were tempted to try elsewhere but decided to work their claim a few more days. To conserve water, they dug a hole for a reservoir. They had dug down about four feet when they struck a mass of black, decomposed silver ore. They did not know what the strange black sand was but figured it was worth washing. They were astonished when the first washing produced a thick coating of gold dust. O'Riley and McLaughlin excitedly continued washing pan after pan until evening.

While they were cleaning up, "Old Pancake" Comstock showed up. Comstock had been searching the area for a stray pony which he had found and was atop of when he stumbled across the Irishmen. Comstock, who had a keen eye for other men's goods, immediately saw the pile of gold dust O'Riley and McLaughlin had produced during the day's washings. Greedy and manipulative, he now set about to steal what he desired.

Comstock told O'Riley and McLaughlin they were on his "ranch." Though Comstock had

nothing to prove it, he claimed he owned the property the Irishmen were mining. Not only were they working his land but they were using his water. Comstock demanded the Irishmen give him and his friend, Manny (Emmanuel) Penrod part of the claim. The Irishmen didn't want trouble and they were unaware how rich their claim was. They agreed to share the claim with Comstock and Penrod. The discovery was called the Ophir. The original locators were filed as Peter O'Riley, Patrick McLaughlin, H.T.P. Comstock, E. Penrod and J.A. (Kentuck) Osborne. Each man was given one sixth of 1,400 feet of ground on the lead; Comstock and Penrod were given an additional 100 feet to split. The entire Ophir claim amounted to 1,500 feet. Comstock and Penrod's additional 100 feet became known as the Mexican or Spanish mine. The site has since been known as Spanish Ravine.

Where previously O'Riley and McLaughlin were making a $1.50-2.00 a day, now they were hauling out $1,000 in gold each day, literally pounds of it. They still did not know what the heavy black sand was and continually cursed it and threw it aside because it interfered with the washing of the gold.

In July, Augustus Harrison, a rancher from the Truckee Meadows, carried a sample of the peculiar black sand to Grass Valley, California where it was assayed. The black sand turned out to be a rich form of silver sulfide and would yield several thousands of dollars of gold and silver per ton.

Harrison tried to keep the discovery quiet but he told a friend, who told a friend, who told a friend and immediately there was a mass exit of California miners for the Washoe Mountains.

At first the new discovery site was called Pleasant Hill, then Mt. Pleasant Point, Ophir and Ophir Diggins. But in November, 1859, James "Old Virginia" Finney, while on a drinking spree with other miners, fell and broke his whisky bottle. "I baptize this ground Virginia," he said, and the town has since been known as Virginia City.

In time the Ophir claim was discovered to be part of a lode of silver ore that stretched nearly continuously three miles and was a hundred feet wide at its broadest point. The Comstock Lode, named after crazy Henry Comstock, ran north and south beneath the eastern base of Mt. Davidson. Virginia City was at the north end of the Lode built on top of the richest portion. Gold Hill was at the southern end. In time, Virginia City, Gold Hill, Silver City and American Flat merged into one mining community known as the Comstock.

Since 1861, the Comstock mines have produced more than 400 million dollars.

Sights to see: The Virginia City cemeteries north of town; the *Territorial Enterprise* building where Mark Twain wrote; Piper's Opera House and the Mark Twain Museum.

Como

This new mining town, with its romantic name is one of the best populated and most promising camps, but as to the mines, I have started out several times to inspect them, but never could get past the brewery
Mark Twain, in the *Territorial Enterprise*

The mining town of Como was located in the Pine Nut mountains 11 miles southeast of Dayton, Nevada. A rugged dirt road leads from the Dayton High School up the Pine Nut Mountains to the site. Mill foundations, mine shafts are all that are left.

Gold was discovered in the Pine Nut mountains June, 1860. A district was formed and a small settlement grew, called Palmyra. About 100 prospectors and miners arrived that summer. There was little further development through 1861.

In 1862 there were additional discoveries a half mile east of Palmyra. A new town site was laid out and named Como.

Como boomed for the next two years. Mining companies were formed and fancy stock was printed in San Francisco. The stock was hustled in Virginia City, 10 miles away, as the crow flies.

Alf Doten, editor of the Gold Hill *News* and a friend of Mark Twain's, was Como's chief publicist. He believed Como would rival Virginia City. Doten was wrong and eventually went broke because of his Como investments.

Doten invited Mark Twain to investigate the Como mines in the summer of 1863. Mark Twain spent three days at the local brewery and never made it to the mines. He wrote in the *Enterprise*, "This new mining town, with its romantic name is one of the best populated and most promising camps, but as to the mines, I have started out several times to inspect them, but never could get past the brewery."

Mark Twain's friend, J.D. Winters, opened several tunnels and built a mill southeast of Como in 1864. Winters shut down the operation at the end of the year because it was unable to cover costs.

By 1865, Como was played out.

The camp was revived twice, 1879-81 and 1902-05. In the 1930's a large mill was built. It ran for a few days when the investors discovered there was no ore to mill. The mill was shut down. Foundations remain.

Steamboat Springs

...the Doctor hesitated a moment, and then fixed up as repulsive a mixture as ever was stirred together in a table-spoon. I swallowed the nauseous mess, and that one meal sufficed me for the space of forty-eight hours. And during that time, I could not have enjoyed a viler taste in my mouth if I had swallowed a slaughterhouse. I lay down with all my clothes on, and slept like a statue from six o'clock until noon. I got up, then, the sickest man that ever yearned to vomit and couldn't. All the dead and decaying matter in nature seemed buried in my stomach, and I "heaved, and retched, and heaved again," but I could not compass a resurrection—my dead would not come forth.
from "Curing A Cold" written at Steamboat Springs

Mark Twain stayed at Steamboat Springs in August, 1863, while trying to get rid of a cold.

He wrote several articles there, including "Curing A Cold," published in the *Enterprise* and the *Golden Era.* Steamboat Springs is located in Washoe Valley 10 miles south of Reno on the east side of U.S. Highway 395.

Steamboat Springs are natural geothermal hot springs. For many years, passing emigrants bathed and camped beside the springs. In the early 1860's, a bath house and hospital were built.

In 1871, after the Virginia and Truckee railroad reached Steamboat Springs, a fine hotel was built to accommodate 50 guests. Included were a drugstore, cottages and 15 sets of baths. This made Steamboat Springs a popular resort, especially for arthritis sufferers. For a year, Steamboat Springs served as an important supply shipping point to Virginia City. But in 1872, when the Virginia and Truckee line was completed between Virginia City and Carson, Steamboat Springs lost its usefulness as a shipping point.

The hot spring resort is currently being restored.

Adaah Isaacs Menken, a well known actress during Twain's day who was best known for her act "Mazeppa" in which Menken appeared in flesh colored tights. She befriended Twain in Virginia City.

Part 3

Hard Times in San Francisco

Arriving in San Francisco in the first week of June, 1864, Twain, took a room at the Occidental Hotel, a place he considered an oasis. There he wrote,

To a Christian who has toiled months and months in Washoe; [Nevada Territory] whose hair bristles from a bed of sand, and whose soul is caked with a cement of alkali dust; whose nostrils know no perfume but the rank odor of sage-brush—and whose eyes know no landscape but barren mountains and desolate plains; where the winds blow, and the sun blisters, and the broken spirit of the contrite heart finds joy and peace only in Limburger cheese and lager beer—unto such a Christian, verily the Occidental Hotel is Heaven on the half shell. He may

even secretly consider it to be Heaven on the entire shell, but his religion teaches a sound Washoe Christian that it would be sacrilege to say it.
The Golden Era, June 26, 1864

In comparison to the barrenness and isolation of Virginia City, Twain found San Francisco invigorating. The city had a population of over 130,000; there were parks, fine restaurants, hundreds of saloons, billiard parlors, high class hotels, many entertaining diversions—musical shows, plays, operas. San Francisco was a seaport more in touch with the outside world;

Below, the Occidental Hotel in San Francisco on Montgomery Street about 1865.

great sailing ships came and went from the bay; water was nearby and there was the salty smell of the sea. The weather was temperate and there was greenery, so lacking in Nevada. Twain fell in love with the city by the bay.

While reporting in Virginia City, Twain had made several trips to San Francisco where he met and became friends with San Franciscan writers and publishers. As early as September, 1863, Twain was submitting articles to the *Golden Era*, a San Franciscan literary journal. The publication of these articles throughout 1863 and 64 combined with Twain's *Enterprise* reputation now enabled him to land a job with the San Francisco *Morning Call*.

Although Twain initially intended to stay in San Francisco a month, during which time he hoped to sell his Hale and Norcross mining stock and return to the East, by June 6, Twain was working full time for the San Francisco *Call*, as its "local items" reporter. Steve Gillis of the *Enterprise* was hired as a compositor and printer. The two young men were roommates

As the *Call's* only reporter, Twain worked from early morning until late at night with a regular beat that included the courts, the police station, and local news. It was monotonous and dull work for a man with great imagination. Twain was paid $40 a week, good pay for the time.

Reporting for the *Call* was not easy for Twain. Unlike working for Joe Goodman and the *Enterprise*, where Twain roamed where he pleased and wrote what he wanted—whether invented or not, George Barnes, the *Call's* editor and co-owner, wanted straight reporting, "just the facts." Twain preferred to interpret events in his own humorous and exaggerated manner. Although the publishers were at first pleased to have a writer with Twain's reputation on the paper, it wasn't long before George Barnes realized that Twain was not the reporter his newspaper needed. Twain was not permitted the professional courtesy of a by-line and his humorous views of life and events, expressed in his local news columns were not greatly appreciated.

In his *Autobiography*, Twain told of his frustration reporting for the *Call* :

After leaving Nevada I was a reporter on the Morning Call *of San Francisco. I was more than that—I was the reporter. There was no other. There was enough work for one and a little over, but not enough for two—according to Mr. Barnes's idea, and he was the proprietor and therefore better situated to know about it than other people.*

By nine in the morning I had to be at the police court for an hour and make a brief history of the squabbles of the night before. They were usually between Irishmen and Irishmen, and Chinamen and Chinamen, with now and then a squabble between the two races for a change. Each day's evidence was substantially a duplicate of the evidence of the day before, therefore the daily performance was killingly monotonous and wearisome...Next we visited the higher courts and made notes of the decisions which had been rendered the day before. All the courts came under the head of "regulars." They were sources of reportorial information which never failed. During the rest of the day we raked the town from end to end, gathered such material as we might, wherewith to fill our required column—and if there were no fires to report we started some.

At night we visited the six theaters, one after another: seven nights in the week, three hundred and sixty-five nights in the year. We remained in each of those places five minutes, got the merest passing glimpse of play and opera, and with that for a text we "wrote up" those plays and operas, as the phrase goes, torturing our souls every night from the beginning of the year to the end of it in the effort to find something to say about those performances which we had not said a couple of hundred times before...

After having been hard at work from nine or ten in the morning until eleven at night scraping material together, I took the pen and spread this muck out in words and phrases and made it cover as much acreage as I could. It was fearful drudgery, soulless drudgery, almost destitute of interest. It was awful slavery for a lazy man, and I was born lazy. I am no

An 1865 view of San Francisco from Nob Hill looking toward San Francisco Bay with the masts of sailing vessels at top.

lazier now than I was forty years ago, but that is because I reached the limit forty years ago...

Despite Barnes' objections, Twain reported the local news in the same casual and humorous way he had on the *Enterprise*. Twain likely got away with it because he wrote his columns close to deadline and Barnes had little time to review and edit them.

For instance, while reporting an accident caused by the driver's fondness for hard liquor, Twain wrote:

A pile of miscellaneous articles was found heaped up at a late hour last night away down somewhere in Harrison street, which attracted the notice of numbers of passers-by, and divers attempts were made to analyze the same without effect, for the reason that no one could tell where to begin, or which one was on top. Two Special Policemen dropped in just then and solved the difficulty, showing a clean inventory of one horse, one buggy, two men and an indefinite amount of liquor. The liquor couldn't be got at to be gauged, consequently the proof of it couldn't be told; the men, though, were good proof that the liquor was there, for they were as drunk as Bacchus and his brother. A fight had been on hand somewhere, and one of the men had been close to it, for his face was painted up in various hues, sky-blue and crimson being prominent. The order of the buggy was inverted, and the horse beyond realizing sense of his condition. The men went with the animal to the station-house, and the animal, with attachments, being set to rights, ambled off to a livery stable on Kearny street.

"Sundries," August 13, 1864, *Call*

Even with such a deadly event as an earth

The early office of the *Daily Morning Call* which burned. The *Call* then moved its offices to the third floor of the Mint Annex at 612 Commercial Street.

quake, Twain found something humorous to say. When an earthquake hit San Francisco, instead of reporting the dull details of the event, Twain wrote it up like this:

...Last night, at twenty minutes to eleven, the regular semi-monthly earthquake, due the night before, arrived twenty-four hours behind time, but it made up for the delay in uncommon and altogether unnecessary energy and enthusiasm. The first effort was so gentle as to move the inexperienced stranger to the expression of contempt... but the second was calculated to move him out of his boots...Up in the third story of this building the sensation we experienced was as if we had been sent for and were mighty anxious to go. The house seemed to waltz from side to side with a quick motion, suggestive of sifting corn meal through a sieve; afterward it rocked grandly to and fro like a prodigious cradle, and in the meantime several persons started downstairs to see if there were anybody in the street so timid as to be frightened at a mere earthquake. The third shock was not important, as compared with the stunner that had just preceded it. That second shock drove people out of the theaters by dozens. At the Metropolitan, we are told that Franks, the comedian, had just come on the stage... and was about to express the unbounded faith he had in May; he paused until the jarring had subsided, and then improved and added force to the text by exclaiming, "It will take more than an earthquake to shake my faith in that woman!" And in that, Franks achieved a sublime triumph over the elements, for he "brought the house down," and the earthquake couldn't.

In one of his more humorous items, Twain reconstructs the police court testimony of a

The Lick House, about 1865, another of Twain's favorite San Franciscan hotels where he lived.

local businessman, his wife and another woman. Watch how Twain turns an ordinary court case into an entertaining drama:

Lena Kahn, otherwise known as Mother Kahn, or the Kahn of Tartary, who is famous in this community for the Police Court as a place of recreation, was on hand there again yesterday morning. She was mixed up in a triangular row, [fight] the sides of the triangle being Mr. Oppenheim, Mrs. Oppenheim, and herself. It appeared from the evidence that she formed the base of the triangle—which is to say, she was at the bottom of the row, and struck the first blow. Moses Levi, being sworn, said he was in the neighborhood, and heard Mrs. Oppenheim scream; knew it was her by the vicious expression she always threw into her screams; saw the defendant (her husband) go into the Tartar's house and gobble up

the partner of his bosom and his business, and rescue her from the jaws of destruction (meaning Mrs. Kahn,) and bring her forth to sport once more—. At this point the lawyer turned off Mr. Levi's gas, which seemed to be degenerating into poetry, and asked him what his occupation was? The Levite said he drove an express wagon. The lawyer—with that sensitiveness to the slightest infringement of the truth, which is so becoming to the profession— inquired severely if he did not sometimes drive the horses also! The wretched witness, thus detected before the multitude in his deep-laid and subtle prevarication, hung his head in silence. His evidence could no longer be respected, and he moved away from the stand...Mrs. Oppenheim next came forward and gave a portion of her testimony in damaged English, and the balance in dark and mysterious German. In the English glimpses of her story it was discernible that she had innocently trespassed upon the domain of the Khan, and had been rudely seized upon in such a manner as to make her arm

The luxurious dining room of the Lick House Hotel. Most of the money that built this hotel and other posh San Franciscan hotels came from the Comstock silver mines.

blue, (she turned up her sleeve and showed the Judge,) and the bruise had grown worse since that day, until at last it was tinged with a ghastly green, (she turned up her sleeve again for impartial judicial inspection,) and instantly after receiving this affront, so humiliating to one of gentle blood, she had been set upon without cause or provocation, and thrown upon the floor and "Licked." This last expression possessed a charm for Mrs. Oppenheim, that no persuasion of Judge or lawyers could induce her to forego, even for the sake of bringing her wrongs into a stronger light...She said the Khan had licked her, and she stuck to it and reiterated with unflinching firmness...she relapsed at last into hopeless German again, and retired within the lines. Mr. Oppenheim then came forward and remained under fire for fifteen minutes, during which time he made it as plain as the disabled condition of his English *would permit him to do, that he was not in anywise to blame...that his wife went out after a warrant for the arrest of the Kahn; that she stopped to "make it up" with the Kahn, and the redoubtable Kahn tackled her; that he was dry-nursing the baby at the time, and when he heard his wife scream, he suspected with a sagacity that did him credit, she wouldn't have "hollered 'dout dere was someding de matter;" therefore he piled the child up in a corner remote from danger, and moved upon the works of the Tartar; she had waltzed into the wife and finished her...*

"The Kahn of Tartary," June 29, 1864, *Call*

Both the Kahn and Mrs. Oppenheim were fined $20 each and let go. In this article, and other articles, Twain's shows his sensitivity to speech and his ability to get it down on paper so that the reader can actually hear the character as if he were there.

In July, Twain and Steve Gillis moved into a rooming house in or near Chinatown. Occasionally they enjoyed raising hell. July 15, 1864,

Montgomery Street from the Eureka Theater about 1864. This area included the famous "Monkey Block" which contained the Occidental Hotel and the Exchange Saloon, where Twain played billiards and swapped jokes. The Block was torn down in 1959 to make way for a parking lot. Notice the horse drawn buses which would later become San Francisco's famous cable cars.

Twain wrote Dan De Quille and gave him an exaggerated account of what their landlady thought of them:

Steve & I have moved our lodgings. Steve did not tell his folks he had moved, & the other day his father went to our room, & finding it locked, he hunted up the old landlady (Frenchwoman,) & asked her where those young men were. She didn't know who he was, & she got her gun off without mincing matters. Said she—"They are gone, thank God—& I hope I may never see them again. I did not know anything about

them, or they never should have entered this house. Do you know, Sir, (dropped her voice to a ghastly confidential tone,) they were a couple of desperate characters from Washoe—gamblers & murderers of the very worst description! I never saw such a countenance as the smallest one had on him. They just took the premises, & lorded it over everything— they didn't care a snap for the rules of the house. One night when they were carrying on in their room with some more roughs, my husband went up to remonstrate with them, & that small man told him to take his head out of the door (pointing a revolver,) because he wanted to shoot in that direction. O, I never saw such creatures. Their room was never vacant long enough to be cleaned up—one of them always went to bed at dark & got up at sunrise, & the other went to bed at sun-rise & got up at dark—& if the chamber-man disturbed them they would just set up in bed & level a pistol at him & tell him to get scarce! They used to bring loads of beer bottles up at midnight, & get drunk, & shout & fire off their pistols in the room, & throw their empty bottles out of the

The corner of Montgomery and Pine Streets, 1865. Streets were still unpaved.

window at the Chinamen below. You'd hear them count One—two—three—fire! & then you'd hear the bottles crash on the China roofs & see the poor Chinamen scatter like flies. O, it was dreadful! They kept a nasty foreign sword & any number of revolvers & bowie knives in their room, & I know that small one must have murdered lots of people. They always had women running to their room—sometimes in broad daylight—bless you, _they_ didn't care. They had no respect for God, man, or the devil. Yes, Sir, they are gone, & the good God was kind to me when He sent them away!"

There, now—what in the hell is the use of wearing away a life-time in building up a good name, if it is to be blown away at a breath by an ignorant foreigner who is ignorant of the pleasant little customs that adorn & beautify a state of high civilization?

The old man told Steve all about it in his dry, unsmiling way, & Steve laughed himself sick over it.

...But don't I want to go to Asia, or somewhere—Oh no, I guess not. I have got the "Gypsy" only in a mild form. It will kill me yet, though.

By mid-September, Twain was tired of working day and night for the _Call_. He told Barnes he would no longer work at night and wrote his mother and sister about his decision September 25:

I am taking life easy, now, and I mean to keep it up for awhile. I don't work at night any more. I told the "Call" folks to pay me $25 a week and let me work only in daylight. So I get up at 10 in the morning, & quit work at 5 or 6 in the afternoon...I have engaged to write for the new literary paper—the "Californian"—same pay I used to receive on the "Golden Era"—one article a week, fifty dollars a

The offices of the *Alta California* newspaper in San Francisco. Twain was hired by the *Alta* to write a series of articles during his 1867 *Quaker City* excursion to the Holy Land. These travel letters became the foundation for *The Innocents Abroad*, Twain's first book published in 1869.

month. I quit the "Era," long ago. It wasn't high-toned enough. I thought that whether I was a literary "jackleg" or not, I wouldn't class myself with that style of people, anyhow. The "Californian" circulates among the highest class of the community, and is the best weekly literary paper in the United States—and I suppose I ought to know.

The Californian, was a mixture of magazine and literary journal started by Bret Harte and Charles Henry Webb in May, 1864. Harte was the major contributor and editor. Harte, who worked for the U.S. Mint in San Francisco, had an office in the Mint Annex. The *Call's* offices were located in the same building on the third floor. The new brick building was at 612 Commercial Street.

Working and writing in the same building, Harte and Twain discovered each other. Though having vastly different natures, they became friends. When both were free they spent time together in Harte's office or at a nearby saloon going over their writings.

Harte was the more experienced writer and took an interest in Twain. He encouraged Twain and taught him how to improve his rough Western humor so that it might reach a wider audience. Though in later years Twain held Harte in contempt for neglecting his wife and family, during the early years of their friendship Twain credited Harte for having tutored him toward his first national success.

One of several versions of the Cliff House where Mark Twain visited in July 1864. He wrote a description of an early morning trip to the Cliff House which was published in the *Golden Era*, July 3, 1864.

By the end of September, 1864 Twain had settled on a "...little quiet street," that was "...full of gardens & shrubbery, & there are none but dwelling houses in it." [letter September 25, 1864] This lodging house was at 32 Minna Street. [*San Francisco Directory*]

Though now working fewer hours for the *Call*, Twain became increasingly bored with the work. It was clear to editor Barnes, and becoming clearer to Twain, he was unsuited for the work.

Though Twain managed to sneak in a satire like, "What A Sky-Rocket Did," which poked fun at a former San Franciscan supervisor, such outlets for his satire in the *Call* were few. George Barnes pleaded with his sluggish reporter to simply get "the facts."

Highly sensitive political articles were also forbidden by Barnes. One day Twain saw a gang of hoodlums chasing and stoning a Chinaman while a policeman stood by, watched and did nothing. It outraged Twain. He wrote a fiery article about the incident and anxiously awaited its publication. But editor George Barnes had different ideas about the article. Twain wrote in his *Autobiography* :

One Sunday afternoon I saw some hoodlums chasing and stoning a Chinaman who was heavily laden with the weekly wash of his Christian customers, and I noticed that a policeman was observing this performance with an amused interest—nothing more. He did not interfere. I wrote up the incident with considerable warmth and holy indignation. Usually I didn't want to read in the morning what I had written the night before; it had come from a torpid heart. But this item had come from a live one. There was fire in it and I believed it was literature—and so I sought for it in the paper the next morning with eagerness. It wasn't there. It wasn't there the next morning, nor the next. I went up to the composing room and found it tucked away among condemned matter on the standing galley. I asked about it. The foreman said Mr. Barnes had found it in a galley proof and ordered its extinction. And Mr. Barnes furnished his reasons—either to me or to the foreman, I don't remember which; but they were commercially sound. He said that the Call *was like the New York* Sun *of that day: it was the washerwoman's paper—that is, it was the paper of the poor; it was the only cheap paper. It gathered its livelihood from the poor and must respect their prejudices or perish. The Irish were the poor. They were the stay and support of the* Morning Call; *without them the* Morning Call *could not survive a month—and they hated Chinamen. Such an assault as I had attempted could rouse the whole Irish hive and seriously damage the paper. The* Call *could not afford to publish articles criticizing hoodlums for stoning...*

...I was loftier forty years ago than I am now and I felt deep shame in being situated as I was—slave of such a journal as the Morning Call. *If I had been still loftier I would have thrown up my berth and gone out and starved, like any other hero. But I had never had any experience. I had dreamed heroism, like everybody, but I had no practice and I didn't know how to begin. I couldn't bear to begin with starving. I had already come near to that once or twice in my life and got no real enjoyment out of remembering about it. I knew I couldn't get another berth if I resigned...Therefore I swallowed my humiliation and stayed where I was...I continued my work but I took not the least interest in it, and naturally there were results.*

Barnes' refusal to publish Twain's Chinese article was the last straw. Despite fear of unemployment, Twain quit the *Call* around October 11. Or Barnes fired him; or they both agreed upon a change. In any case, Twain later admitted he wasn't totally blameless. In the last weeks of reporting he had,

....neglected my duties and became about as worthless, as a reporter for a brisk newspaper. And at last one of the proprietors took me aside, with a charity I still remember with considerable respect, and gave me the opportunity to resign my berth and so save myself the disgrace of dismissal.

Chapter 58 *Roughing It*

Years later, George Barnes remembered his

heart to heart talk with Twain:

"Mark, do you know what I think about you as a local reporter?"

"Well, what's your thought?"

"That you are out of your element in the routine of the position, that you are capable of better things in literature."

Mark looked up with a queer twinkle in his eye.

"Oh, ya-a-s, I see. You mean to say I don't suit you."

"Well, to be candid, that's about the size of it."

"Ya-a-s. Well, I'm surprised you didn't find out five months ago."

There was a hearty laugh. He was told his unfitness for the place was discovered soon after he entered on it...

Clemens of the "Call," Mark Twain In San Francisco

George Barnes recalled Twain was a, "good general writer and correspondent, ... [but he] made but an indifferent reporter. He only played at itemizing." He, "parted from THE CALL people on the most friendly terms...admitting his reportorial shortcomings and expressing surprise they were not sooner discovered." ["Mark Twain. As He Was Known during His Stay on the Pacific Slope," George E. Barnes, *Morning Call*, April 17, 1887.]

Two things helped Twain quit the *Call*. He was writing articles for the *Californian*, which paid him well, allowed him to express himself, required less work, and provided him with the prestige he desired. Second, Twain was toying with the idea of writing a book, and naturally, he would need time for that. He wrote his brother Orion, September 28:

I would commence on my book, but (mind, this is a secret, & must not be mentioned,) Steve & I are getting things ready for his wedding, which will take place on the 24th Oct. He will marry Miss Emmelina Russ, who is worth $100,000, & what is much better, is a good, sensible girl & will make an

The interior of the Palace Hotel mid-1870's, another of San Francisco's prestigious hotels.

excellent wife. Of course I shall "stand up" with Steve, at the nuptials, as chief mourner. We shall take a bridal tour of a week's duration...

I only get $12 an article for the Californian *but you see it makes my wages up to what they were on the* Call, *when I worked at night, & the paper has an exalted reputation in the east, & is liberally copied from by papers like the* Home Journal...

Well Mollie [Orion's wife] *I do go to church. How's that?*

As soon as this wedding business is over, I believe I will send to you for the files, & begin my book.

Ironically, Twain did not start his book, which apparently was to be about life on the Mississippi. Nor did Orion send him his "files," a collection of Twain's articles published in Nevada and California newspapers, which Orion

had saved. These articles, and letters Twain wrote to his mother and sister while living in Nevada and California, would be the basis for parts of Mark Twain's second book, *Roughing It*, which Twain wrote after he had left the West for good.

Twain's only income now came from the publication of articles he wrote for *The Californian*. Between November 12 and December 3rd, 1864, Twain published three articles for which he was paid $12 each. Including his partial October *Call* salary, Twain's total income from October 11, to December 3rd, was about $61. It was the least Twain had earned in two years and it bothered him. He wrote of this time:

For two months my sole occupation was avoiding acquaintances; for during that time I did not earn a penny, or buy an article of any kind, or pay my board. I became very adept at "slinking." I slunk from back street to back street, I slunk away from approaching faces that looked familiar, I slunk to my meals, ate them humbly and with a mute apology for every mouthful I robbed my generous landlady of, and at midnight, after wanderings that were but slinkings away from cheerfulness and light, I slunk to my bed. I felt meaner, and lowlier and more despicable than the worms. During all this time I had but one piece of money—a silver ten cent piece—and I held to it and would not spend it on any account, lest the consciousness coming strong upon me that I was entirely penniless, might suggest suicide. I had pawned every thing but the clothes I had on; so I clung to my dime desperately, till it was smooth with handling.

Chapter 59 *Roughing It*

In late November, Steve Gillis, a small but fierce fighter, was involved in a barroom brawl with Big Jim Casey, a Barbary Coast saloon keeper. Gillis brained Casey with a beer pitcher and nearly killed him. Gillis was arrested for assault with intent to kill; Twain posted Gillis' $500 bond.

When Casey's condition worsened and it looked like he would die, Gillis figured it was in his best interest to leave San Francisco until the trouble blew over. Gillis returned to Virginia City and went back to work for the *Enterprise*. Gillis' skipping town, left Twain responsible for Gillis' $500 bond. Twain did not have the money and that meant Twain himself might end up in jail.

There is some speculation as to exactly why Twain left San Francisco in December, 1864. Albert Bigelow Paine, Twain's first biographer, believed Twain left town both to escape paying Gillis' bond and to avoid trouble with the police following Twain's publication of articles about San Francisco police corruption. But these articles were not published until October, 1865, long after Twain had returned from Jackass Hill.

Gillis' bond trouble may have been part of Twain's decision to leave. But a lack of income and a need of rest are more plausible reasons.

At the time Twain left San Francisco for Jackass Hill, he was nearly broke and needed a place to stay. Twain admitted in a letter that he was unable to pay his landlady for room and board. Even after he returned from Jackass Hill, he spent more than a year repaying past debts. Besides being broke, Twain was just plain tired. For four months he had worked hard as a reporter for the *Call*. While writing for the paper and for two months afterward, Twain had written a number of articles for literary papers attempting to establish himself as a free-lance writer. After quitting the *Call*, his struggle to earn a living as a writer and his failure to earn enough to cover living expenses, increased Twain's mental stress. Any serious writer who has pounded out writing daily, foregoing the luxury of a paycheck at the end of the week, understands the frustration when he is unable to pay for basic living expenses. Broke and tired, Twain wanted a rest.

Twain's decision to leave town fits his life-long pattern of intense work periods followed by long rests. The rests were often spent traveling.

"By and by, an old friend of mine, a miner, came down from one of the decayed mining camps of Tuolumne, [County] California, and I went back with him," wrote Twain [Chapter 60 *Roughing It*] . The old friend was Jim Gillis, Steve's older brother. Jim Gillis suggested Mark Twain stay with him on Jackass Hill until the San Francisco trouble ended.

Twain left San Francisco around December 1 and arrived on Jackass Hill, December 4, 1864. While roaming the Sierra foothills with Jim Gillis in search of gold, Twain would unearth a treasure that would change his life.

San Francisco

After the sagebrush and alkali deserts of Washoe [Nevada], San Francisco was Paradise to me. I lived at the best hotel, exhibited my clothes in the most conspicuous places, infested the opera...I had longed to be a butterfly, and I was one at last. I attended private parties in sumptuous evening dress, simpered and aired my graces like a born beau, and polkaed and schottisched with a step peculiar to myself—and the kangaroo. In a word, I kept the due state of a man worth a hundred thousand dollars...and likely to reach absolute affluence when that silver-mine sale should be ultimately achieved in the East.

...And then—all of a sudden, out went the bottom and everything and everybody went to ruin and destruction! The wreck was complete...I was an early beggar and a thorough one...I the cheerful idiot that had been squandering money like water...had not now as much as fifty dollars when I gathered together my various debts and paid them. I removed from the hotel to a very private boardinghouse. I took a reporter's berth and went to work.

Chapter 58 *Roughing It*

Mark Twain made his first trip to San Francisco from Virginia City in early May, 1863 with his friend and fellow reporter, Clement T. Rice, whom Twain had dubbed the Unreliable. The two spent nearly a month in San Francisco before returning to Virginia City. They partied at the Occidental Hotel, ate at the Lick House, played billiards at the Exchange saloon and visited the Cliff House.

Twain returned to San Francisco in September for another month. May 29, 1864 he left Virginia City for San Francisco after allegedly challenging a rival editor to a duel. Duels were against Nevada law. Friends encouraged Twain to get out of Dodge until the dust settled.

In June, 1864, Twain moved into San Francisco's prestigious Occidental Hotel on Montgomery Street in what was known as the Montgomery Block or the Monkey Block. This area was the commercial district of San Francisco known as Wall Street west. One of Twain's favorite haunts was the Exchange Saloon where Twain played billiards and swapped jokes with fellow reporters and friends. Another haunt was a Turkish bath where Twain allegedly met the original Tom Sawyer, the owner of the place.

Though Twain wrote in *Roughing It* that he spent some time playing the butterfly and spending his money foolishly, within a week of arriving in San Francisco he was working for the San Franciso *Call*. He reported for the paper until October 11 when he quit or was fired. He then attempted to earn a living writing articles for San Franciscan literary magazines, the *Golden Era* and the *Californian*.

He left San Francisco December 1, 1864 for a three month stay on Jackass Hill and returned to the Occidental Hotel around February 26, 1865. He remained in San Francisco until March 7, 1866, then sailed aboard the *Ajax* to the Sandwich (Hawaiian) Islands as a correspondent for the Sacramento *Union*. Twain stayed on the Islands for five months. By August 13 he was back in San Francisco.

Two months later, October 2, 1866, Twain gave his first big lecture on the Sandwich Islands at Tom Maguire's Academy of Music in San Francisco. Twain had been encouraged by friends to give his lecture career a try. Twain rented the hall, placed ads in the papers, printed posters and plastered them around town. With about two thousands people in attendance, Twain's second paid-for lecture was a great success and kicked off his long career as one of America's favorite speakers.

December 15, 1866 Twain sailed from San Francisco for New York. He returned to San Francisco in March 1868 where he continued writing the first draft of *The Innocents Abroad*. June 23rd he wrote his publisher, "The book is finished, & I think it will do. It will make more than 600 pages, but I shall reduce it at sea." Twain meant he would edit portions of the manuscript on his voyage back to New York. In a letter to Mary Fairbanks June 17, Twain wrote that the *Innocents* manuscript was already 2,343 pages, a "mountain" of manuscript. Twain was writing eleven to twelve hours a day from midnight until late morning, averaging three thousand words a day.

July 6, 1868 Mark Twain sailed from San Francisco Bay and left San Francisco and the Far West for good.

San Francisco is built on high sand dunes at the head of a peninsula that shoves its head into the Pacific Ocean at the mouth of the Golden Gate. The Golden Gate is the largest land opening along the pacific coast for a thousand miles. The Golden Gate opens into the San Francisco Bay into which pour the waters of the Sacramento and San Joaquin Rivers. For thousands of years the only inhabitants were the Ohlones, a sub Indian tribe of the Coast Miwok. The Ohlones fed themselves on oysters and left evidence of their delight in this food by leaving huge shell piles on the shores along the bay; the largest is located at Coyote Hills in southern Alameda County.

Everything went all right for the Ohlones and their brother Coast Miwoks until the Spanish fleet showed up in 1769. In 1776 Juan Bautista de Anza and a Catholic priest marched up the peninsula from Sonora, Mexico. They saw the beauty of the wind swept tip of the peninsula and said to themselves,"Grab it," which they did. The Spaniards built a fortress on a high hill above the Golden Gate and called it the Presidio. The Spanish built five missions around the bay, rounded up the Ohlones, shoved Catholicism down their throats and put them to work growing vegetables. And then the Spanish generously gave the Ohlones some of their European diseases. About five thousand dead Ohlones are planted in unmarked graves at San Francisco's Mission Dolores at Our Lady of Sorrows—a good name for the place. San Francisco was then known as Yerba Buena.

In the 1840's the Yankees began infesting Yerba Buena, coming south from the Oregon Trail. Yerba Buena was still owned by the Mexican government. The Americans fixed that when John C. Fremont in 1846 raised a flag and declared California's independence from Mexico.

Then the Yankees changed the name of Yerba Buena to San Francisco after the Bay.

When gold was discovered in 1848 at Sutter's Mill at Coloma on the American River, the Yankees poured out of the East on ships and wagons, on horses and on foot. They piled into San Francisco before making the inland trip up the Sacramento River to Sacramento and into the Sierra foothills. The increase in population meant an increase in the need for food, supplies and building materials. It was all shipped into San Francisco and shipped inland from there. San Francisco boomed and a city quickly took shape upon the sand dunes. In 1852 the United States Government built a mint in San Francisco.

By the 1860's, the gold rush was over and San Francisco had become a stable city. With the gold and silver strike on the Comstock Lode in 1859, money continued to pour into San Francisco which had become the financial and power center on the West Coast.

Through the 1860's, 70's and 80's, thousands of people from many nations settled in San Francisco. The city became cosmopolitan with a large number of Asians who huddled together in Chinatown.

Sights to see: There is so much to see in this seven by seven mile city you could write a book about it. The truth is, many guide books have been written about San Francisco. I suggest you buy Barry Parr's *San Francisco and the Bay Area*, published by Compass American Guides out of Oakland, California. Now sells for $12.95. Some of the places I suggest to see are Fisherman's Wharf at Pier 39, where the sea lions congregate in the autumn and winter. There's Chinatown of course. Spend some time walking through the crowded streets at night— and take the side streets. There you will find hundreds of Chinese restaurants. Be dangerous. Find one that is filled with Chinese *patrons* and take a seat. My family and I did this once; the food was great and we had a wonderful time, the children google-eyed the live fish and lobsters in the glass tank prior to the latter meeting their Maker.

Get away from the crowds and traffic and visit Golden Gate park, one of America's finest. There you will find trees and flowers and open space. There's lots to do and see. Visit the Children's Playground, the Conservatory of Flowers, the science museum at the California Academy of Sciences, Steinhart Aquarium, with 14,000 fish, crabs, turtles, dolphins, etc.; Watis Hall of Man has displays of Polynesian, Melanesian, Asian and other peoples, and there's Morrison Planetarium. There are several other museums and displays. Explore. Have fun.

For those who are into history, try the Wells Fargo History Room at 420 Montgomery Street in the heart of Wall Street west. There you will find an actual Wells Fargo stagecoach and lots of photos and memorabilia from Well's Fargo's days in the Wild West.

Sorry to say, much of Mark Twain's San-Francisco has been destroyed by various fires and earthquakes. The worst was the earthquake and fire of 1906. More damage was done by the fire than by the earthquake. Those seeking the old San Francisco should head toward Jackson Square which is found across Washington Street, north of the Transamerica Pyramid building. Here along Pacific Street were located a string of saloons, whorehouses, dives and dance joints known as the horrific and perverted Barbary Coast. This was Twain's old stomping ground; some buildings date back to the 1860's. Here in the Barbary Coast Steve Gillis brained Big Jim Casey with a beer pitcher and nearly killed Casey. This assault caused Gillis and Twain to flee San Francisco in December, 1864.

Below, Pacific Street of the notorious Barbary Coast. It was in this neigborhood that Steve Gillis nearly killed Big Jim Casey.

Part 4

Escape to Jackass Hill

This statue of Mark Twain is in Utica Park in Angel's Camp, Calaveras County and memorializes Twain's discovery of the "Jumping Frog" story at Angel's Hotel. "The Celebrated Jumping Frog of Calaveras County" became Mark Twain's first well known national and international story.

Jim Gillis' home was a one room plank cabin on Jackass Hill. The Hill was named "Jackass," in the late 1840's because of the large numbers of jackasses teamsters parked on the Hill on their supply trips through the Mother Lode mining camps.

Jim Gillis, and his partner, Dick Stoker, had mining claims all over the Hill. Today the reddish-brown earth of Jackass is pock-marked with a myriad of bomb-shell holes where the Gillises and Stoker, and miners afterward, dug their "pocket" mines. There are a few mine shafts with the usual piles of rock and sand. But for the most part, miners worked shallow pockets rather than incur the labor, expense and danger of underground mining.

When Twain visited Jackass Hill in 1864, the Gold Rush had been dead more than a decade. Other mining camps in California and Nevada had drawn most of the living elsewhere. Miners and merchants had left behind clapboard and brick towns like corpses with their hearts cut out. Jackass Gulch (Tuttletown) had become one of those once thriving places that had nearly been deserted when Twain visited. In 1864, Jackass Gulch was no longer a village, just a stone general store, "Swerer's Store," the two story wooden Tuttletown Hotel, built in 1852, and a solitary saloon. First called Mormon Gulch, Jackass Gulch had been established in 1848 at the break of the California Gold Rush.

Jim Gillis [1830-1907] was the eldest of the four Gillis brothers. He was thirty-four when Mark Twain stayed with him at Jackass Hill. Twain was twenty-nine. Mark Twain wrote of Jim Gillis as being an "old friend," at the time he visited Gillis on Jackass Hill. The two likely

Left, Jim Gillis, elder brother of Steve Gillis. Photo taken near the turn of the century. Gillis had invited Twain to stay with him on Jackass Hill in December, 1864. Right, Richard "Dick" Stoker, Gillis' mining partner and friend. Twain wrote about both men in _Roughing It_.

first met in San Francisco through Steve Gillis.

It was Jim Gillis, who, while Twain stayed with him, improvised the story of Dick Baker and his cat, Tom Quartz, one evening by the fireplace. Mark Twain told his own version in _Roughing It_, Chapter 61. Twain based the character Dick Baker on Gillis' roommate, Dick Stoker, Jacob Richard Stoker [1818-96] a forty-six year old bachelor whom Twain described in _Roughing It_ as, "...one of the gentlest spirits that ever bore its patient cross in a weary exile...grave and simple...gray as a rat, earnest, thoughtful, slenderly educated, slouchily dressed and clay-soiled, but his heart was finer metal than any gold his shovel ever brought to light—that any, indeed, that ever was mined or minted." Gillis also created the drama, "The Tragedy of the Burning Shame," which the boys acted out in the cabin and Twain later used in _Huckleberry Finn_.

During Twain's three month stay, Billy Gillis, Jim's youngest brother, also lived in the cabin. Jim, Billy Gillis and Dick Stoker earned meager livings through "pocket" gold mining.

Twain explained this curious human endeavor in his _Autobiography_:

A "pocket" is a concentration of gold dust in one little spot on a mountain side; it is close to the surface; the rains wash its particles down the mountain side and they spread, fan-shape, wider and wider as they go. The pocket-miner washes a pan of dirt, finds a speck or two of gold in it, makes a step to the right or to the left, washes another pan, finds another speck or two, and goes on washing to the right and to the left until he knows when he has reached both limits of the fan by the best of circumstantial evidence, to wit—that his pan washings furnish no longer the speck of gold. The rest of the work is easy—he washes along up the mountain side, tracing the narrowing fan by his washings, and at last reaches the gold deposit. It may contain only a few hundred dollars, which he can take out with a couple of dips of his shovel; also it may contain a concentrated treasure worth a fortune. It is the fortune he is after and he will seek it with a never-perishing hope as long as he lives.

These friends of mine [Jim Gillis and Dick Stoker] had been seeking that fortune daily for eighteen years; they had never found it but they were not at all discouraged; they were quite sure they would find it some day. During the three months that I was with them they found nothing, but we had a fascinating and delightful good time trying. Not long after I left, a greaser (Mexican) came loafing along and found a pocket with a hundred and twenty-five thousand dollars in it on a slope which our boys had never happened to explore.

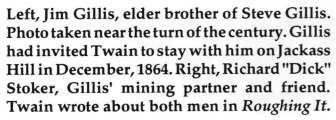

This is the original Gillis cabin on Jackass Hill which is believed to have burned down around 1900. The cabin was gone when Twain's first biographer, Albert Bigelow Paine visited the Hill in 1907.

Of the pocket miners around Jackass Hill, Twain wrote in Chapter 60 of *Roughing It*:

There are not now more than twenty pocket miners in that entire little region. I think I know every one of them personally. I have known one of them to hunt patiently about the hillsides every day for eight months without finding gold enough to make a snuffbox—his grocery bill running up relentlessly all the time—and then find a pocket and take out of it two thousands dollars in two hours, and go and pay up every cent of his indebtedness, then enter on a dazzling spree that finished the last of his treasure before the night was gone. And the next day he bought his groceries on credit as usual, and shouldered his pan and shovel and went off to the hills

hunting pockets again happy and content. This is the most fascinating of all the different kinds of mining, and furnishes a very handsome percentage of victims to the lunatic asylum.

...The hogs are good pocket hunters. All the summer they root around the bushes, and turn up a thousand little piles of dirt, and then the miners long for the rains; for the rains beat upon these little piles and wash them down and expose the gold, possibly right over a pocket. Two pockets were found this way by the same man in one day. One had five thousand dollars in it and the other eight thousand dollars. That man could appreciate it, for he hadn't had a cent for about a year.

Mark Twain tried his hand at pocket mining with Jim, Billy Gillis and Dick Stoker. But he, like the others, was not successful. He wrote:

At the end of two months we had never "struck" a pocket. We had panned up and down the hillsides till they looked plowed like a field; we could have put

This is a replica of the original Gillis cabin built in 1922 under the direction of Bill Gillis. However, both cabins have differences. The new cabin's planks run vertically and the new cabin seems smaller. The chimney of the original cabin had fallen by 1900.

in a crop of grain, then, but there would have been no way to get it to market. We got many good "prospects," but when the gold gave out in the pan and we dug down, hoping and longing, we found only emptiness— the pocket that should have been there was as barren as our own. At last we shouldered our pans and shovels and struck out over the hills to try new localities. We prospected around Angel's Camp, in Calaveras County, during three weeks, but had no success. Then we wandered on foot among the mountains, sleeping under trees at night, for the weather was mild, but still we remained as centless as the last rose of summer. That is a poor joke, but it is in pathetic harmony with the circumstances, since we were so poor ourselves. In accordance with the custom of the country, our door had always stood open and our board welcome to tramping miners— they drifted along nearly every day, dumped their paust shovels by the threshold, and took "potluck"

with us—and now on our tramp we never found cold hospitality.

Our wanderings were wide and in many directions...

Chapter 61 *Roughing It*

Mark Twain spent December, 1864 with Jim Gillis and Dick Stoker at the Jackass Hill cabin. He wrote,

We lived in a small cabin on a verdant hillside, and there were not five other cabins in view over the wide expanse of hill and forest. Yet a flourishing city of two or three thousand population had occupied this grassy dead solitude during the flush times of twelve or fifteen years before, and where our cabin stood had once been the heart of the teeming hive, the center of the city...The grassy slopes were as green and smooth and desolate of life as if they had never been disturbed. The mere handful of miners still remaining had seen the town spring up, spread, grow, and flourish in its pride; and they had seen it sicken and die, and pass away like a dream. With it their hopes had died, and their zest of life. They had long resigned themselves to their exile and ceased to correspond with their distant friends or turn long-

ing eyes toward their early homes. They had accepted banishment, forgotten the world and been forgotten of the world. They were far from telegraphs and railroads, and they stood, as it were, in a living grave, dead to the events that stirred the globe's great populations, dead to the common interests of men, isolated and outcast from brotherhood with their kind. It was the most singular, and almost the most touching and melancholy exile that fancy can imagine. One of my associates in this locality, for two or three months, was a man who had had a university education; but now for eighteen years he had decayed there by inches, a bearded, rough-clad, clay-stained miner, and at times, among his sighings and soliloquizings, he unconsciously interjected vaguely remembered Latin and Greek sentences—dead and musty tongues, meet vehicles for the thoughts of one whose dreams were all of the past, whose life was a failure; a tired man, burdened with the present and indifferent to the future; a man without ties, hopes, interests, waiting for rest and the end.

Chapter 60 *Roughing It*

In between pocket mining explorations, the boys walked down the hill to Tuttletown for groceries at Swerer's Store and drinks, conversation and billiards at Tuttletown's one saloon.

Most of the time they hung around the Jackass Hill cabin swapping yarns, reading Byron, Shakespeare, Dickens and doing odd jobs around the cabin. Twain is said to have read and written beneath a large oak tree beside the cabin. The tree has since died. A large stump remains near the original cabin site.

On New Year's Eve, 1864, the boys hiked over Table Mountain to Vallecito, in Calaveras County. Vallecito, Spanish for "little valley," had been a roaring mining camp in the early 1850's. When Twain visited, Vallecito was a quiet town with a general store and a single church. A bell once used to call the miners to worship, hung in an old oak tree beside the church. A hillside west of town held the remains of the miners who had died during the early days. Many were Mexican.

January 3rd, Twain and Jim Gillis returned to Jackass Hill by making a loop through Angel's Camp, then heading south crossing the Stanislaus River at Robinson's Ferry. Back on Jackass Hill, the days were spent as before reading and telling each other stories.

Mark Twain and Jim Gillis remained on Jackass Hill until January 22nd. Then they returned to Angel's Camp by way of Carson Hill. They apparently went to Angel's Camp to work Jim's pocket claim located in the nearby hills.

But their plans to prospect at Angel's Camp were fouled when two weeks of winter rains began on January 23rd. Twain and Gillis were forced to take a hotel room at Angel's Camp and broke up the monotony by going down to the "Frenchman's" for breakfast and dinner. The Frenchman's food was nothing to write home about. Twain wrote in his notebook, "beans & coffee only for breakfast & dinner every day at the French Restaurant at Angel's—bad, weak coffee—J [Jim] told waiter must made mistake—he asked for cafe—this was day-before-yesterday's dishwater..."

Trapped indoors while it rained, Twain made these notes in *Notebook 4*:

Jan. 23, 1865—Angels—Rainy, stormy—Beans and dishwater for breakfast at the Frenchman's, dishwater & beans for dinner, & both articles warmed over for supper.

24th—Rained all day—meals as before

25—Same as above

26th—Rain, beans & dishwater—tapidaro [a leather cover from a Mexican stirrup] *beefsteak for a change—no use, could not bite it.*

27th—Same old diet—same old weather—went out to the "pocket" claim—had to rush back.

28th—Rain & wind all day & all night. Chili beans & dishwater three times to-day, as usual, & some kind of "slum" which the Frenchman called "hash." Hash be d—d.

29th—The old, old thing. We shall have to stand the weather but as J [Jim] says, we won't stand this dishwater & beans any longer, by G—

30th Jan.—Moved to the new hotel, just opened—

Robinson's Ferry on the Stanislaus River. Mark Twain and Jim Gillis used the ferry to cross the river on their way back from Angel's Camp. The ferry was replaced by a bridge on Highway 49 in 1910. This site along with the town of Melones was flooded by waters of the New Melones Reservoir in 1978.

good fare, & coffee that a Christian may drink without jeopardizing his eternal soul.

The "new hotel," or rather, their new lodgings, was likely Angel's Hotel at the southern end of Angel's Camp. A canvass hotel in 1851, the tent was replaced by a one story wooden building, then by a stone building in 1855. In 1857, a second story was added. A saloon with a billiards table was located on the first floor on Main Street. The hotel stands today.

By February 6, two weeks of seasonal winter rains ended. Now the days were warm with fair nights. For the next two weeks, Twain, Gillis and Stoker spent their days combing the hillsides near Angel's Camp for pocket mines. As usual, Twain sat under an oak tree and watched while Jim and Dick dug the ground and washed it in their pans. The boys camped beneath the oak trees spending their nights around the campfire, and as Twain wrote in his notebook, "Camp meeting exhorting, slapping on back till make saddle boils." They were lazy, carefree days Mark Twain fondly looked back to the rest of his life.

Around February 20th, the boys returned to Angel's Camp. At this time they once again visited the saloon at Angel's Hotel. Here a dull bartender named Ben Coon, told Mark Twain a story that would change his life.

Twain made a brief notation of the discovery in *Notebook 4*:

Coleman with his jumping frog—bet stranger $50— stranger had no frog, & C [Coleman] got him one— in the meantime stranger filled C's [Coleman's] *frog full of shot* [lead pellets] *& he couldn't jump— the stranger's frog won.*

Years later, Twain wrote a note in blue ink over this notation, "Wrote this story ["Jim Smiley and His Jumping Frog"] for Artemus [Ward]—his idiot publisher, Carleton gave it to [Henry] Clapp's *Saturday Press.*"

About the time Twain was on Jackass Hill, Ward wrote Twain at his San Francisco address and asked Twain to submit a story for his upcoming book, *Artemus Ward; His Travels.* Months later, Twain submitted the "Jumping Frog," to Ward's publisher in October, too late to be included in Ward's book. Ward's publisher would pass on the "Jumping Frog" to another publisher.

In March 18, 1865, in "An Unbiased Criticism," published in the *Californian,* Twain wrote that the person who first told him the "Jumping Frog" story was an ex-corporal [Ben] Coon, "a nice baldheaded man at Angel's Camp." Twain later depicted the narrator of the "Jumping Frog" as:

...a dull person, and ignorant; he had no gift as a story-teller, and no invention; in his mouth this episode was merely history—history and statistics; and the gravest sort of history, too, he was entirely serious, for he was dealing with what to him were austere facts, and they interested him solely because they were facts; he was drawing on his memory, not his mind; he saw no humor in his tale, neither did his listeners; neither he nor they ever smiled or laughed,... "Private History of the 'Jumping Frog' Story," *North American Review,* April, 1894

Dull or not, Ben Coon gave Mark Twain the idea for a short story that would do more for his career and fame, than all the articles he had written in the past two years.

February 20th, 1865, Mark Twain left Angel's Camp and returned to Jackass Hill with Jim Gillis and Dick Stoker. Two days later he borrowed a horse and rode to Copperopolis, 12 miles west of Angel's Camp, where he stayed for two days. February 25th, he left Copperopolis by stage for San Francisco by way of Stockton.

Jackass Hill

We lived in a small cabin on a verdant hillside, and there were not five other cabins in view over the wide expanse of hill and forest. Yet a flourishing city of two or three thousand population had occupied this grassy dead solitude during the flush times of twelve or fifteen years before, and where our cabin stood had once been the heart of the teeming hive, the center of the city...

Chapter 60 *Roughing It*

Mark Twain stayed with Jim Gillis on Jackass Hill from December 4, 1864, to February 23, 1865. The old oak tree which Mark Twain is said to have sat under and written by, died in 1942. A stump remains.

A mile north of Tuttletown a branch road leads 1 mile up to Jackass Hill. A road marker on California Highway 49 points the way to "Mark Twain's Cabin," as it is called today, located on Jackass Hill.

Jackass Hill was the stopping place for packers carrying supplies to the local mining camps. Often as many as 200 jackasses were parked on the hill whose hee-hawing suggested the name Jackass Hill.

The Mark Twain Cabin is a replica of the original Jim Gillis cabin which was destroyed around 1900. The replica was built about 300 feet west of the original cabin site.

Coarse gold was found here in a 100 square feet of ground producing $10,000 in gold.

Tuttletown (Jackass Gulch)

...It was the most singular, and almost the most touching and melancholy exile that fancy can imagine. One of my associates in this locality, for two or three months, was a man who had a university education; but now for eighteen years he had decayed there by inches, a bearded, rough-clad, clay-stained miner, and at times, among his sighings and soliloquizings, he unconsciously interjected vaguely

Above, Tuttletown (Jackass Gulch) in the 1920's. Tuttletown Hotel and restaurant are on the left. Swerer's store is on the right. Here Mark Twain and Jim Gillis traded December, 1864 to February, 1865.

remembered Latin and Greek sentences—dead and musty tongues, meet vehicles for the thoughts of one whose dreams were all of the past, whose life was a failure; a tired man, burdened with the present and indifferent to the future; a man without ties, hopes, interests, waiting for rest and the end.

Chapter 60 *Roughing It*

Mark Twain visited Tuttletown and Jackass Hill from December 4, 1864 to February 23, 1865. A replica of the Gillis cabin is located two miles from the Tuttletown site on Jackass Hill. The Tuttletown Hotel and Swerer's General store no longer exist.

Tuttletown is located in Tuolumne County, California, 8 miles north of Sonora on California Highway 49.

First called Mormon Gulch in 1848, the name was changed to Tuttletown after Judge Tuttle who built a cabin and became the leading citizen. The right wing of the Tuttletown Hotel was built in 1852, as was the stone building known as "Swerer's Store," where Mark Twain and Jim Gillis bought supplies and played billiards. Tuttletown was known as Jackass Gulch by local miners.

Sights to see: Sonora, and Columbia State Park outside Sonora, a mining camp dating back to the California Gold Rush.

Angel's Camp

Dined at the Frenchman's, in order to let Dick see how he does things. Had Hellfire soup & the old regular beans & dishwater. The Frenchman has 4 kinds of soup which he furnishes to customers only on great occasions. They are popularly known among the borders as Hellfire, General Debility, Insanity & Sudden Death, but it is not possible to describe them.

Mark Twain, *Notebook 4*

Swerer's store in Tuttletown in the 1920's. Today nothing remains at Tuttletown but the corner stone of this building.

Mark Twain spent two weeks in Angel's Camp in January, 1865. While visiting Angel's Hotel, he first heard a dull bartender, Ben Coon, relate the story about a jumping frog. Twain's version, "Jim Smiley and his Jumping Frog," published the following autumn, became an instant national success and kicked off Twain's international career.

Angel's Camp is located on California Highway 49 in the western Sierra foothills 25 miles north of Sonora.

George Angel, for whom the town is named, came west in 1848. He built a trading post where Angel's Creek and Dry Creek meet. The place came to be known as Angel's Camp and grew fast during the exciting years of the Gold Rush in the early 1850's.

One of the most important gold strikes was made by a miner called Raspberry. His curious discovery is the stuff of legends. Raspberry was either cleaning or loading his muzzle-loaded rifle, when the steel rod became jammed. Unable to pull it out, he decided to shoot it out and pulled the trigger. The rod shot into a rock formation and broke it up. Low and behold, when Raspberry went to retrieve his rod, he found the busted-up rock glittered with gold. Raspberry took nearly $10,000 from the claim in a matter of days. He continued working the claim and made a fortune.

Angel's Hotel, where Mark Twain first heard the Jumping Frog story, still stands. The old jail house is behind it. Angel's mine, one of the most profitable in the area, is located across from the Catholic Church. Only the mill foundations remain. A museum at the north end of town has a collection of minerals, mining era tools and antiques.

Angel's Camp today is best known for its County Fair in May when the annual jumping

Angel's Hotel in Angel's Camp today. It was here that Mark Twain heard Ben Coon tell the tale of the "Jumping Frog of Calaveras County."

frog contest is held. Each year thousands of contestants arrive with frogs of all sizes. In order to qualify for the contest, a frog must be four inches in length from nose to tail. The frog that jumps the farthest in three consecutive jumps, wins. The owner is lauded with riches an honor.

There is a monument to the frog on Main Street and a statue of Mark Twain in Utica Park in Angel's Camp on California Highway 49.

Some believe that Angel's Camp was the true setting for Bret Harte's "Luck of Roaring Camp." Harte taught school at nearby La Grange in 1855 before he moved on to Robinson's Ferry on the Stanislaus River. Harte became partners with several miners who tried their luck as far north as Angel's Camp.

Harte did not like life as a miner and spent little time in the mining camps. He thought the Sierra foothills were, "hard, ugly, unwashed, vulgar and lawless." During the short time he was there, he was more a visitor than a partici-

pant. He remained a city man with clean boiled shirts, patent leather shoes, unable to relate to the miner's life and drams. Mark Twain considered Harte's knowledge of the California mining camps superficial.

Vallecito

New Year's night 1865, at Vallecito, magnificent lunar rainbow, first appearing at 8 PM—moon at first quarter—very light drizzling rain.

Mark Twain *Notebook 4*

Mark Twain spent New Year's eve, 1864 at Vallecito and there began his *Notebook 4* January 1, 1865.

Vallecito is located a few miles east of Angel's Camp on State Highway 4.

Vallecito, Spanish for "little valley," was settled in 1850 by Mexican miners. The settlement boomed in 1852 when a rich gold strike was made. The boom was short lived.

There are several well kept cemeteries with graves of the early Mexican miners. The Dinkelspiel store and the Wells Fargo Express office remain. The bell that called the miners to worship hangs by itself next to the church.

Copperopolis

Mark Twain arrived in Copperopolis the evening of February 23, 1865, after his stay on Jackass Hill. He had hoped to attend a ball that was canceled. The following day he visited the Union Copper Mine, descending 30 feet down the dark mine shaft. February 25 he left Copperopolis by stage for San Francisco. Mark Twain wrote in this *Notebook 4*, Copperopolis, "is a pretty town & has about 1000 inhabitants. D—d poor hotel, but if this bad luck will let up on me I will be in Stockton at noon tomorrow & in San Francisco before midnight."

Copperopolis is 13 miles southwest of Altaville on Highway 4. From Stockton take Highway 4, 37 miles east to Copperopolis.

From 1860 to 1867 Copperopolis was one of the largest copper producers in the United States and served as an important supplier of copper during the Civil War. During these years the town had a population of around 2,000, two churches, four hotels, many shops and stores and a weekly newspaper, the Copperopolis *Courier*. Copperopolis also supplied much of the copper used during World Wars I and II.

At the south end of town there are several buildings from the early years. The largest, a brick building, was the Federal Armory and headquarters for the Copperopolis Blues during the Civil War. Next door to the old Armory are the warehouse and office buildings of the Copperopolis Consolidated Mining Company. The head frames and mine dumps are across the street.

Below a hotel at Copperopolis where Twain may have stayed in February, 1865.

Part 5

Correspondent to Hawaii, Europe and Back West

An unusually wild and serious looking Mark Twain as he struggled in the West to make a name for himself as roaming correspondent and speaker.

Arriving back in San Francisco in early February, Twain took a room at the Occidental Hotel, his old haunt. There he picked up his mail, some of which had been held for several months. Among the mail was Artemus Ward's letter which requested Twain to submit a story for Ward's upcoming book. For unknown reasons, Twain did not immediately respond to Ward's request.

Twain continued contributing articles to the *Californian* for $12 each. By mid-June he was writing daily correspondent letters for the *Enterprise* from which he earned $100 a month.

Twain's *Californian* writings managed to attract attention in the East when the New York *Round Table* acknowledged Twain as a humorist on the rise. October 18, 1865, the San Francisco *Dramatic Chronicle* [today's *San Francisco Chronicle*] reprinted the *Round Table's* comments in a clip, "Recognized." The editor of the *Round Table* wrote:

The foremost among the merry gentlemen of the California press, as far as we have been able to judge, is one who signs himself "Mark Twain." Of his real name we are ignorant, but his style resembles that of "John Phoenix" more nearly than any other, and some things we have seen from his pen would do honor to the memory of even that chieftain among humorists. He is, we believe, quite a young man, and has not written a great deal. Perhaps, if he will husband his resources and not kill with overwork the mental goose that has given us these golden eggs, he may one day take rank among the brightest of our wits.

Sacramento in the 1870's. Mark Twain called it the "City of Saloons."

Twain was encouraged by the *Round Table's* attention and wrote his brother about the notice:

...I have had a "call" to literature, of a low order—i.e. humorous. It is nothing to be proud of, but it is my strongest suit, & if I were to listen to that maxim of stern duty which says that to do right you must multiply the one or the two or the three talents which the Almighty entrusts to your keeping, I would long ago have ceased to meddle with things for which I was by nature unfitted & turned my attention to seriously scribbling to excite the laughter of God's creatures. Poor, pitiful business! Though the Almighty did His part by me—for the talent is a mighty engine when supplied with the steam of education,—which I have not got, & so its pistons & cylinders & shafts move feebly & for a holiday show & are useless for any good purpose...You see in me a talent for humorous writing, & urge me to cultivate it...now, when editors of standard literary papers in the distant east give me high praise, & who do not know me & cannot of course be blinded by the glamour of partiality, that I really begin to believe there must be something in it...I will drop all trifling, & sighing after vain impossibilities, & strive for a fame—unworthy & evanescent though it must of necessity be—if you will record your promise to go hence to the States & preach the gospel when circumstances shall enable you to do so? I am in earnest. Shall it be so?

Letter to Orion and Mollie Clemens, October 19 and 20, 1865

Though earning a fair living as a full time writer, Twain admitted in the same letter he was still in debt.

In October, 1865, eight months after Artemus Ward's request, Twain mailed Ward his version of the story he first heard Ben Coon tell at Angel's Camp, "Jim Smiley and His Jumping Frog." Ward received the story October 18, 1865, too late for publication. Ward's publisher, without Mark Twain's consent, passed the story on to Henry Clapp, editor of the New York *Saturday Press.* Clapp published the "Jumping Frog," in the *Saturday Press,* November 18, 1865.

Like many incidents in Mark Twain's life, the

San Francisco waterfront and wharves in the late 1860's. Sailing ships with tall masts and steamers came and went from the Bay. Twain sailed from here several times.

publication of the "Jumping Frog," in the *Saturday Press*, proved remarkably fortunate. As was the common custom of the time, the story was copied and reprinted by numerous newspapers throughout America and Europe. This caused the "Jumping Frog " to reach a wider audience than it would have, had it first been published in Artemus Ward's book, which ironically, died a quick, silent death.

When "Jim Smiley and His Jumping Frog," was published it was enormously successful and received high praise in New York and elsewhere. The San Francisco *Alta California* noted the tale's success when its New York correspondent, Richard L. Ogden wrote,

Mark Twain's story in the Saturday Press *of November 18, called* "Jim Smiley and His Jumping Frog," *has set all New York in a roar. I have been asked fifty times about it and its author, and the papers are copying it far and near. It is voted the best thing of the day. Cannot the* Californian *afford to keep Mark all to itself? It should not let him scintillate so widely without first being filtered through the California press.*

Despite the "Jumping Frog's" success, Twain was somewhat disturbed by it. He wrote his mother and sister:

...To think that after writing many an article a man might be excused for thinking tolerably good, those New York people should single out a villainous backwoods sketch to compliment me on!—"Jim Smiley and His Jumping Frog"—a squib which would never have been written but to please Artemus Ward, & then it reached New York too late to appear in his book [Artemus Ward; His Travels].
Letter to Jane Lampton Clemens

The Apollo Saloon in Sacramento around 1870.

On March 7, 1866, Mark Twain sailed from San Francisco aboard the *Ajax* to the Sandwich (Hawaiian) Islands as a special correspondent for the Sacramento *Union*. He intended to stay on the Islands a month, but stayed five months. During this time he gathered material for twenty-five correspondent letters, most of which he wrote while on the Islands. The Sandwich Islands letters were published in the Sacramento *Union*; they were very popular and increased Twain's esteem in California. Twain intended to publish these letters as a book about the Sandwich Islands. The letters eventually were the foundation for Chapters 62-77 of *Roughing It*.

It was while Twain was in the Sandwich Islands that he happened to grab a major scoop which would further increase his reputation in California. The *Hornet*, a ship on its way from New York had caught fire near the Galapagos Islands and sank. Fifteen men had managed to survive. They spent forty-three days in an open boat with ten days supply of food and water. Eleven men managed to make it to Honolulu by June 21.

Twain was the only American reporter on the islands and he saw the sinking of the *Hornet* and the survival of its crew as an important news story. He wanted to interview the survivors at the hospital. Problem was, Twain, who had been roaming the islands by horseback, had developed awful boils on his buttocks and was confined to bed.

Enter Anson Burlingame, American minister to China. Twain had just met Burlingame and his son, who considered Twain somewhat of a celebrity for his "Jumping Frog" success, in Honolulu. Burlingame had just arrived from San Francisco on his way to China. Burlingame ordered men to haul Twain on a stretcher to the hospital in order to interview the *Hornet* survivors. While Burlingame asked questions, Twain took notes. Twain wrote the story that night and dramatically threw the manuscript aboard a departing vessel the following morning. Or so Twain claimed. The *Hornet* scoop made the front page of the *Union* in three columns. It was

Tom Maguire's Academy of Music in San Francisco. Twain gave his first professional lecture here October 2, 1866 followed by a speaking tour of California and Nevada mining towns. Tom Maguire also owned Maguire's Opera House in Virginia City where Twain spoke.

the first and most complete coverage of the disaster. Twain later published the story in *Harper's* as "Forty-three Days in an Open Boat."

Twain left the Islands July 19 and by August 13, 1866 he was back in San Francisco. During the last half of the month, he finished writing the rest of his Sandwich Island letters for the Sacramento *Union*. He also began submitting articles for the New York *Weekly Review*. Again in September, the *Union* hired Twain to cover the California State Agricultural Society at Sacramento.

October 2, 1866, with the encouragement of friends, Twain gave his second humorous lec-

ture about the Sandwich Islands at Maguire's Academy of Music in San Francisco. [His first lecture was given in Carson City, January 27, 1863, as a benefit for the First Presbyterian Church.] The lecture was a great success, attended by the best in town and well reviewed by local papers. This led Twain to a quick lecture tour of several California and Nevada mining towns. His old *Enterprise* pal, Denis McCarthy, acted as Twain's manager. Twain and McCarthy "raided" Marysville, Sacramento, Nevada City, Grass Valley, Red Dog, and You Bet. In Nevada they hit Virginia City, Gold Hill, Silver City, Dayton, Washoe City and Carson City.

Twain lectured in Virginia City on October 31. Though Twain had left Virginia City in May, 1864 under a cloud, he was welcomed back with opened arms. Piper's Opera House, Twain's old haunt, was crammed for the lecture. Twain's hour and a half talk brought the house down.

Hamilton Hall in Grass Valley where Mark Twain spoke October 23, 1866 and April 21, 1868.

Twain returned to San Francisco in November. December 15, 1866, he sailed for New York. He had been hired by the San Francisco *Alta California* as a traveling correspondent. The *Alta* wrote,

"Mark Twain" goes off on his journey over the world as the Traveling Correspondent of the ALTA CALIFORNIA, not stinted as to time, place or direction—writing his weekly letter on such subjects and from such places as will best suit him; but we may say that he will first visit the home of his youth—St. Louis—thence through the principal cities to the Atlantic seaboard again, crossing the ocean to visit the "Universal Exposition" at Paris, through Italy, the Mediterranean, India, China, Japan, and back to San Francisco by the China Mail Steamship line. That his letters will be read with

interest needs no assurance from us—his reputation has been made here in California, and his great ability is well known; but he has been known principally as a humorist, while he really has no superior as a descriptive writer—a keen observer of men and their surroundings—and we feel confident his letters to the ALTA, from his new field of observation will give him world-wide reputation.

"Mark Twain's Farewell," San Francisco *Alta California*, December 15, 1866

Twain eventually sailed from New York, June 8, 1867 aboard the *Quaker City* for Europe and the Holy Land. During this trip he wrote a series of travel letters for the *Alta California* .

When Twain returned to America in November, 1867, he settled in Washington, D.C. at Nevada Senator William Stewart's apartment where he began writing *The Innocents Abroad*, based on the *Quaker City* letters. During the ensuing months a dispute arose between Twain and the *Alta California* regarding Twain's use of

Little remains of the old mining town of Red Dog near Grass Valley where Mark Twain spoke October 24, 1866.

the letters in his book. Twain sailed to California in March, 1868 to secure their rights. Back in California, Twain quickly persuaded the *Alta's* publishers, who had copyrighted the letters, to allow him to use the letters as the basis for the *Innocents*.

In April, 1868 Twain gave lectures on his travels to the Holy Land in San Francisco and in Virginia City, April 27. Piper's Opera House was not full but Twain's lecture was much applauded.

Through May and June, Twain continued writing his first draft of *The Innocents Abroad* in San Francisco, completing it by the end of June.

July 6, 1868, Mark Twain sailed from San Francisco and returned to New York. He had left California and Nevada for good.

In 1905, Robert Fulton invited Mark Twain to Reno to honor him. Mark Twain was then sixty-nine and unable to accept Fulton's invitation.

But he wrote Fulton a moving letter May 24, 1905:

Dear Mr. Fulton:

I remember, as if it were yesterday, that when I disembarked from the overland stage in front of the Ormsby in Carson City in August, 1861, I was not expecting to be asked to come again. I was tired, discouraged, white with alkali dust, and did not know anybody; and if you had said then, "cheer up, desolate stranger, don't be downhearted—pass on, and come again in 1905, " you cannot think how grateful I would have been and how gladly I would have closed the contract...

...I thank you sincerely for the invitation; and with you, all Reno, and if I were a few years younger, I would accept it, and promptly. I would go. I would let somebody else do the oration, but, as for me, I would talk—just talk. I would renew my youth; and talk—and talk—and talk—and have the time of my life! I would march the unforgettable antiques by, and name their names, and give them reverent "Hail-and-farewell" as they passed: Goodman, McCarthy, Gillis, Curry, Baldwin, Winters,

The interior of Piper's Opera House in Virginia City around 1900. This is the third version. Though Twain did not actually speak in this building, the opera house gives visitors a feel of what the old opera houses may have been like. Piper's is open for tours during the summer.

Howard, Nye, Stewart, Neely Johnson, Hal Clayton, North, Root, and my brother—upon whom be peace!—and then the desperadoes, who made life a joy and the "Slaughterhouse" a precious possession: Sam Brown, Farmer Pete, Bill Mayfield, Six-fingered Jake, Jack Williams, and the rest of the crimson discipleship...Believe me, I would start a resurrection it would do you more good to look at than the next one will...

Those were the days!—those old ones. They will come no more. Youth will come no more. They were so full to the brim with the wine of life; there have been no others like them. It chokes me up to think of them. Would you like me to come out there and cry?

It would not besteem my white head.

Good-bye. I drink to you all. Have a good time—and take an old man's blessing.

Twain's years in Nevada and California led to the writing and publication of his first two books: *The Innocents Abroad,* published in 1869, a literary and financial success. It was followed in 1872 by, *Roughing It,* a well written, hilarious account of Twain's experiences in the Far West. Included in *Roughing It,* were many of the characters and people Twain had known in the West.

In the ensuing years "Jim Smiley and His Jumping Frog," the little story which kicked off Mark Twain's international career, became known as "The Celebrated Jumping Frog of Calaveras County," and "The Notorious Jumping Frog of Calaveras County."

Though Mark Twain often spoke and wrote of returning to California and Nevada, he never did.

John Millian, the 35 year old Frenchman who murdered Julia Bulette, prostitute, in Virginia City. Twain attended Millian's hanging April 24, 1868 while in Virginia City to speak. Twain wrote an account of the hanging for the *Territorial Enterprise*.

Sacramento

...we come to the eternal summer of Sacramento. One never sees summer clothing or mosquitoes in San Francisco—but they can be found in Sacramento. Not always and unvaryingly, but about one hundred and forty-three months out of twelve years, perhaps. Flowers bloom here, always, the reader can easily believe—people suffer and sweat, and swear, morning, noon and night, and wear out their stanchest energies fanning themselves.

Chapter 56 *Roughing It*

I arrived in the City of Saloons this morning at 3 o'clock, in company with several other disreputable characters, on board the good steamer Antelope...*I know I am departing from usage in calling Sacramento the City of Saloons instead of the City of the Plains, but I have my justification...You can shut your eyes and march into the first door you come to*

and call for a drink, and chances are that you will get it...In addition to the saloons, there are quite a number of mercantile houses and private dwellings.
Territorial Enterprise February 25, 1866

The Sacramento *Union* employed Twain as an independent writer on several occasions. In March, 1866, he was hired to write a series of articles about his trip to the Sandwich (Hawaiian Islands.) This trip led to the scoop of the *Hornet*, a clipper ship that sank off the Hawaiian Islands, whose survivors spent forty-three days in an open boat. Twain's scoop helped solidify his West Coast career as an important journalist. Twain's letters for the Sacramento *Union* would become the basis for Chapters 62-77 of *Roughing It*. Twain made several trips to Sacramento and lectured there in 1866 and 1868.

Sacramento is located in northern California in the Sacramento Valley where the Sacramento and American Rivers converge. It is intersected by I-80, I-5, and U.S. Highways 50 and 99.

In 1839, John Augustus Sutter, a Swiss immigrant, sailed two ships up the Sacramento River and parked them where the Sacramento and American Rivers converge. He, one German, a Belgian, an Irishman, an Indian and ten Hawaiians, unloaded two brass cannons, a bunch of supplies and began a settlement Sutter called New Helvetia. A rich settlement in America was the fulfillment of Sutter's dream.

Sutter had been granted Mexican citizenship and 50,000 acres of land in the Sacramento Valley. The Mexicans wanted to keep Americans from settling in the Central Valley and they thought Sutter would help them achieve their goal. Within days of the grant, the Hawaiian crew was making adobe bricks and clearing the land for farming. Adobe buildings were built with grass roofs. Two years later the buildings were surrounded by walls three feet thick enclosing a settlement 500 feet long and 150 feet wide. The place came to be known as Sutter's Fort.

Stories were published in American newspapers about Sutter's blossoming colony. By 1841, Easterners were struggling over the Sierra Nevada and winding up on the doorsteps of Sutter's Fort. Some sailed up the Sacramento River from San Francisco; some came down from Oregon. In need of skilled workers, Sutter hired many. The American population exploded. Just what the Mexicans didn't want.

Sutter hired James Marshall, a carpenter, to help build a sawmill on the American River 35 miles east of the fort at Coloma. In 1848, while building the mill, Marshall discovered gold in the millrace. The California Gold Rush started immediately after.

In 1849 thousands swarmed into California and headed for Sutter's Fort and the Sierra foothills. Sutter's Fort became an important supply point and way station between San Francisco and the Sierra mining camps. A city grew around the fort and became known as Sacramento City, named after the Rio del Sacramento, or Spanish for the "River of the Sacrament."

By 1848, Sacramento City's population reached 14,000. By 1854, Sacramento had grown to such a size and influence, the people elected Sacramento as the capitol of California and so it remains to this day.

By 1860, the Gold Rush had petered out. Miners returned from the foothills and settled in the Sacramento Valley where they built farms, planted fruit trees and acres of vegetables. Many became wealthy feeding the hungry city of San Francisco.

Passage of the Pacific Railroad Act in 1860 led to legislation in 1862 which authorized the government to loan money to build the Central Pacific Railroad. Theodore Judah, Collis Huntington, Mark Hopkins, Charles Crocker and Leland Stanford began constructing a railroad that would cross the Sierra, Nevada and reach Promontory Point, Utah, in 1869. The building of the railroad helped Sacramento to grow. The Sacramento Embarcadero became a beehive of activity as rails and engines were unloaded.

Sights to see: Sutter's Fort and Indian Mu-

seum on K Street; the State Capitol; State Library; Old Town and the Railroad Museum at Old Town and Coloma State Park at Coloma where Marshall's discovery of gold kicked off the Gold Rush. An annual jazz festival is held every spring in Sacramento.

Grass Valley and Nevada City

Mark Twain gave lectures at Grass Valley and Nevada City during his October, 1866 and April, 1868 lecture tours of California and Nevada mining towns. The two towns are 4 miles apart. They are located in northern California, approximately 45 miles northeast of Sacramento on California Highway 49, the Gold Country highway. To reach the towns drive northeast on Interstate 80 from Sacramento to Auburn, another quaint old mining town. Then head north on Highway 49, 24 miles to Grass Valley. On both lecture trips, Twain had "raided" Grass Valley and Nevada City after lectures at Marysville, 28 miles west of Grass Valley.

Grass Valley was perhaps the most prosperous Gold Rush mining town in California, and its vast bodies of gold ore were the longest lasting. Mining continued in Grass Valley into the 1950's. Unlike other Western slope mining towns whose main claim to fame were placer deposits—loose gold separated from the dirt by washing the dirt with water, Grass Valley had mines with large bodies of hard rock bearing gold. Because of the hard rock mines, mining at Grass Valley was more complex and more costly, requiring heavy machinery for deep mining. This type of mining also required important technical skills and know-how. Where individual placer miners could make it on their own with pick and shovel and hit-and-miss surface deposits, they did not have the knowledge or the finances for deep hard rock mining. Therefore, heavily financed mining companies did most of the mining at Grass Valley and Nevada City. The companies were run well and profitable. Due to the richness of the gold mines and the well financed mining companies, Grass Valley, unlike other

Washoe City in Washoe Valley north of Carson City about 1865. Mark Twain spoke here November 8, 1866. Little remains of the original town site.

Motherlode mining towns was able to support a large number of suppliers and businesses; the economy was more diverse and stronger. Today the town still feels solid and substantial although local businesses depend heavily on tourists.

The story of the gold discovery at Grass Valley is not unlike many of the accidental discovery tales you hear throughout the Motherlode mining towns. If we can believe the story, George Knight, while chasing after his cow one moonlit night in 1849, happened to slam his toe into a chunk of gold bearing quartz that glittered with flakes of gold in the moonlight. Knight carried the quartz home and quickly hand-milled the ore, discovering the quartz was rich with gold. The discovery drew hundreds of miners to the site in the summer of

1849. A mill was built which produced 4 million dollars between 1850 and 1857. Other mining companies set up shop and dug deep mines within a mile or two of the site: Empire, Pennsylvania, North Star and others. Today the Empire Mine State Historic Park is a good place to learn about deep mining; there's lots of mining equipment there to marvel at.

Both Grass Valley and Nevada City still have many buildings which date back to the early mining days. The small, wooden houses and narrow winding streets remind you more of a New England town, rather than some place in California.

Nevada City, just north of Grass Valley, was first settled in 1849 by placer gold miners who worked the placers along Deer Creek. As with Grass Valley, much of the gold had to be gotten by deep, hard rock mining. One of the most interesting places is James Ott's Assay Office. It was Ott who first assayed the strange silver ore from Virginia City and told the world of its extraordinary richness.

Some of the early pioneers are buried in the Washoe City cemetery along U.S. Highway 395 in Washoe City.

Sights to see at Grass Valley : Empire Mine State Park; the Lola Montez home at the corner of Mill and Walsh streets, now the Nevada County Arts Council. Montez was a famous actress of the 19th century. Tourist information can be found at the Grass Valley Chamber of Commerce located in the old *Union* newspaper office at 151 Mill Street. There's the Nevada County Historical Mining Museum in Boston Ravine. The museum has the largest Pelton wheel in the world. The museum is open 11 a.m. to 5 p.m. in the summer; and open Saturday through Monday the rest of the year.

At Nevada City pick up a walking tour guide at the Chamber of Commerce at 132 Main Street. There are lots of old Victorian buildings, houses and churches with tall steeples to see. Along Broad Street, the main thoroughfare, there are the National Hotel, the New York Hotel, the Methodist Church, the old brick Firehouse No. 2, and farther out on West Broad Street you'll find the pioneer cemetery. Check out the American Victorian Museum on Commercial Street if

you are into Victorian artifacts. You'll also find buildings dating back to the 1860's in the old Chinese section along Commercial Street.

Washoe City

Mark Twain stayed at Washoe City with Tom Fitch in November, 1866 to present his Sandwich Island lecture. Fitch was a friend, a journalist and lawyer. Twain, Fitch and others had established the *Weekly Occidental*, in Virginia City in February, 1864. It died a quick death. The Washoe City stop was part of Mark Twain's first lecture tour in 1866 which included, San Francisco, Sacramento, several California gold mining camps, Dayton, Silver City, Gold Hill and Virginia City, Nevada.

Twain also stayed at the nearby ranch house of Theodore Winters, a friend. Winters' former house still stands on the east side of U.S. Highway 395. Winter's Ranch, a bed and breakfast, is located across the street.

The Washoe City town site is located 18 miles south of Reno and 12 miles north of Carson City, in Washoe Valley on the northwest shore of Washoe Lake. The site can be reached from Reno or Carson by taking U.S. Highway 395. The Washoe City cemetery is well preserved

Odeon Hall at Dayton, Nevada near Virginia City. Twain likely spoke here November 7, 1866 and in late April, 1868.

and located on the west side of the highway. One large commercial brick building stands on the east side. There are a number of old houses.

When nearby Virginia City boomed in 1860, there was a great need for timber for the underground mines and lumber for houses and commercial buildings. Timber was available in the Sierra Nevada mountains above Washoe Valley. Located on Washoe Creek, Washoe City had plenty of water to operate sawmills. Due to the lack of water in Virginia City, stamp mills were also built in Washoe City to crush Comstock ores . The ore was hauled from Virginia City in wagons.

In addition, there were farms in Washoe Valley which produced vegetables and meat for Virginia City. Washoe City was the nearest shipping point. Washoe City was located on the busy route between Carson City and the Truckee Meadows, now called Reno.

Washoe City seemed to magically appear early in 1861. In November, 1861, it was made the Washoe county seat. Judges, lawyers, doctors and a dentist moved in. Soon there were stores, saloons, a bath house, livery stables, feed yards, sawmills and stamp mills. In October, 1862, the Washoe *Times* began publishing. A school and a hospital were built. In 1863, the county constructed a brick courthouse and jail.

By 1865, the town had a population of around 6,000. But as the Virginia City mines floundered at the end of the first boom, the town's economy suffered. In 1869, when the Virginia and Truckee railroad completed a line from Virginia City to the Carson River, stamp mills were built along the Carson River. The ease and less expensive shipment of ores from Virginia City to the Carson mills, hurt the Washoe City mills. The town was crippled.

By 1880, Washoe City had no more than 200 people. In 1894, the post office was closed.

Top left, Mark Twain not long before his death. Top right, Frank Fuller former Governor of Utah who managed Twain in New York City. Fuller helped pull off the successful Cooper's Union debut of Twain in New York City. Bottom, Twain with his family at their Hartford home.

The Robbing of Mark Twain

Following Mark Twain's lecture at Gold Hill, Nevada on the evening of November 10, 1866, Mark Twain was robbed on the Divide between Gold Hill and Virginia City. It was a practical joke instigated by Steve Gillis, Twain's good friend and former *Enterprise* associate. As Twain and his manager Denis McCarthy walked over the Divide in the fierce cold, six men approached in the darkness. Mark Twain reported next day in the *Enterprise* that their leader, a small man, said:

"Stand and deliver!"
I said, "My son, your arguments are powerful. Take what I have, but uncock the pistol."
The young man uncocked that infamous pistol (but he requested three other gentleman to present theirs at my head) and then he took all the money I had (only $20 or $25) and my watch. Then he said to one of this party:
"Beauregard, go through that man!" meaning Mac—and the distinguished rebel did go through Mac. Then the little captain said:
"Stonewall Jackson, seat these men by the roadside and hide yourself; if they move within five minutes, blow their brains out!"
"All right, sir!" said Stonewall. Then the party (six in number) started toward Virginia City and disappeared.

What bothered Mark most about the robbery was the theft of his gold watch. The following day he published a plea in the *Enterprise*:

Now I want to write you road agents as follows: My watch was given me by Judge Sandy Baldwin and Theodore Winters, and I value it above anything else I own. If you will send that to me (to the Enterprise office or to any prominent man in San Francisco), you may keep the money and welcome. You know, you got all the money Mac had—and Mac is an orphan—and besides, the money he had belonged to me. Adieu, my romantic friends.

Dan De Quille later wrote of the robbery:

The robbery had been planned by Mark's old friends as a sort of advertising dodge. It was intended to create sympathy for him, and by having him deliver a second lecture in Virginia City afford the people an opportunity of redeeming the good name of the Comstock. He would have had a rousing benefit, and after all was over his agent would have returned his watch and money. Of course it would not have done to ask Mark his consent to be robbed for this purpose... His friends meant well, but like other schemes of mice and men this particular one failed to work. Mark was too "hot" to be handled and when at last it was explained to him that the robbery was a sham affair he became still hotter—he boiled over with wrath.

His money and watch were returned to him after he had taken his seat in the stage, and his friends begged him to remain, but he refused to disembark. Upon observing some of his friends of the police force engaged in violent demonstrations of mirth, he turned his attention to them and fired a broadside of anathemas as the stage rolled away. Had he kept cool he would have had a benefit that would have put at least a thousand dollars in his pocket, for the papers had made a great sensation of the robbery.

    " Reporting With Mark Twain"

What made Twain even angrier, he got a severe cold from having to stand so long in the bad weather on the Divide.

On his return lecture trip to Virginia City in April, 1868, Twain wired ahead to Joe Goodman, "I am doing well, having crossed one divide without getting robbed anyway," which showed he had forgiven his friends their former transgression.

Conclusion

This book has no value unless I can share something with you that will encourage you in your life or speak to you where you live.

I have spent much of the last seven years studying Mark Twain's life in Nevada and California. In concentrating on one period of a man's life, it is wise to study periods prior and after. In time, when you have learned enough, you begin to judgments on a man's life as if you were God. You try not to do this, but it can't be helped. You look at a man's life from beginning to end, all you've learned that he said and did and ask yourself: What has this man taught me about living? What did he believe was true? On what values did he base his life? What made him successful? And in discovering the answers to these questions, a writer may pass on to you what he has learned .

Mark Twain was extraordinarily clever. Not just clever with his wit and humor, but with the way he got the reader's attention, and then subtly laid out what he really wanted to say. Twain knew he must entertain readers and he worked hard to do so. What often comes off as casual, off-the-cuff humorous comments, were the results of years of practice and work.

But Twain wanted to do more than entertain. He wanted to teach. And he did. Though he writes in his preface to Hu*ckleberry Finn*, "persons attempting to find a moral...will be banished," we can be certain that there is a moral in this book as there are in all of Twain's serious writing.

In *Huckleberry Finn* Mark Twain was the first American writer with the courage to teach his generation that Jim, the Negro slave, is a human being with feelings, human enough to agonize over the wife and children that have been torn from him and sold by greedy, insensitive white people. That a black man could be a human being with feelings was a new idea to some of Twain's generation, as it is to some of ours. And Twain, who wrote and published *Huck Finn* twenty years after the bitter Civil War, displayed considerable bravery in making this point. And to learn, as I write this, that alleged educated people in America are still calling for the banishment of this book from American libraries is astonishing. And why? Over one word: "nigger, " which Huck uses to describe Jim. It was the right word for Twain to put in Huck's mouth. "Nigger." It is an ugly, unkind word. But it is the word people of Twain's generation used to describe a black man; it was *the* word Twain needed to use to illustrate how white people of Twain's day saw black people. Isn't this the point Twain was trying to make?

Which brings me to this: Twain was a preacher. He was quick to notice injustice and his pen was sure to illuminate any injustice with venom and brilliance. As I have pointed out in this book, Twain's beginnings as a writer with a moral voice began in the West in Virginia City and Carson City and continued the rest of his life.

Where did this moral voice come from? In part it came from his mother, a stoic Presbyterian who believed in Christ and His teachings and rigorously instilled those values in her son, Samuel. Clemens' mother was a woman who would go out of her way to protect the low and needy. She had a strong sense of justice. But she also had a sense of humor.

I am blazingly convinced that it was Twain's Sunday school lessons in the little Presbyterian Church at Hannibal that helped lay the foundation for Twain's moral values. These Christian values were to be the basis for all of Twain's serious endeavors as a person and writer. Twain's private and published writings show us that he had much knowledge and understanding of the Bible. This says to me, for whatever reasons, Twain had spent considerable time mulling over the various issues presented in the Bible. Though Twain was certainly skeptical about certain sections of scripture, one senses his reverence and appreciation for the wisdom one may find in this book. And I am astonished that most Twain scholars entirely avoid this issue.

Not only was Twain a preacher of moral values costumed in satire and wit, but he was a prophet. What is a prophet's job? It is to shows us our errors and help restore us to right values and right living. If not restore, then, to remind us of what is right and wrong, good and evil, just and unjust. A prophet tries to keeps us human, decent, right thinking.

Whether it is in *The Innocents Abroad, Huckleberry Finn,* his *Autobiography,* or in his hundreds of letters, if we listen, we hear Twain the preacher/prophet saying again and again: Tell the truth. Be kind to one another. Don't let bad people to do bad things to good people. Pretense is nonsense. It is the condition of the heart that matters. *All of these are values found in the Mosaic Law and the New Testament :* truth, love, justice, the importance of a right heart.

It is ironic that during Twain Western years, when he was living more wildly than he would ever live, that he began inserting his trademark Biblical allusions in his writings and personal letters.

What made Mark Twain successful?

First, he was endowed with an extraordinary gift for language.

Second, he was sensitive and keenly observant.

Third, he had the ability to see himself honestly, and thereby see human beings as we really are.

Fourth, he was able to articulate his understanding of human nature with wit and satire.

Fifth, he worked hard and was committed to becoming a better writer, a better person, more educated.

Sixth, he had a mother who taught him right values which he was able to adopt.

Seventh, he was a practical and shrewd marketer of his writing and speaking talents.

And eighth, regardless of what some scholars and critics may write or believe, I believe Mark Twain revered God and understood we are ever under His eyes and hands. Something mysterious and good happens to us when we acknowledge our Creator.

Skeptical of portions of the Bible?

Yes, Twain was.

Astonished by the way alleged Christians treated each other and their non-believing brothers?

Yes, Twain was. And terrifically angered by false Christians who did not behave with the love and compassion of their Savior.

In later years, seeing his mission to teach human beings to be kind was impossible and possibly a failure, Mark Twain grew increasingly pessimistic and cynical about the "damned human race." This leads me to believe that he may have not accepted a basic Christian belief: that all men are sinners, all sick with the same disease, all needing the same cure: Christ. Missing this, Twain blamed human beings for being what we can't help being.

Twain often spoke of himself as unsaved, unbelieving, a doubter, a sinner, beyond help, but when you read his personal letters, you discover a man who held an unswerving conviction that God existed, whose ways may be difficult to understand, but still a God in charge of the show. And Twain, of all wise men, was wise enough to give that God his due—despite his lifelong arguments with Him.

In his last years following the deaths of his daughters Susy and Jean, and the death in 1904 of his wife Livy, Mark Twain became bitter. He was angry that a good God could have taken such fine people out of his life. In the *dark* writings of his last years, Twain's anger and bitterness are there for us to see and feel. It is easy to understand, that a man who had won so much in life and been given so much, now having lost the people he loved and needed, would grow bitter.

I do not see these final attacks on God as Mark Twain's lack of faith, agnosticism or atheism. Mark Twain had fought hard on the side of right most of his adult life; he had accomplished more than most elementary school drop-outs will ever attempt. He was tired, lonely, depressed and physically ill; his soul was sick. We have all been there. Or will be. It is easy to sympathize.

From time to time I've speculated about what happened when Twain met God face to face. I've wondered if Twain's final attacks on God's authority were even too much for His mercy.

I would like to believe that God forgave Mark Twain. For I believe that a man who accepts Christ as his Savior can't ever escape that decision. Some will say that Twain never believed in Christ as Savior but Twain's own words—particularly in his love letters to Livy before they married—support my conclusion that Twain did believe in Christ as God.

My feeling is, for whatever it may matter, that like Twain, we may become angry at God, argue with Him, question Him, at times lose faith and turn away, but I believe God never entirely turns away from us. It is not His nature. I believe God was there for Mark Twain, even in his last days when he was lonely, bitter and perhaps most angry with God. For as Twain himself wrote, he may have been a fool, but then, he was God's fool.

Author's Suggested Reading List

If you want to learn more about Mark Twain's life in the West, I suggest you read other books in the author's series. *Mark Twain: His Adventures at Aurora and Mono Lake*, details Clemens' mining experiences at Unionville and Aurora, Nevada. *Mark Twain: His Life in Virginia City, Nevada*, covers Twain's twenty-one months as a reporter for the *Territorial Enterprise*. *Mark Twain: Jackass Hill and the Jumping Frog*, begins with Mark Twain's departure from Virginia City, covers his five months as reporter for the San Francisco *Call* and his three month stay on Jackass Hill. During this latter time Twain discovered the story of the Jumping Frog.

Paul Fatout's *Mark Twain in Virginia City*, published in 1964, was the first detailed work on Twain's years as a reporter for the *Enterprise*. The book reads well, and it is thorough. Fatout gives considerable attention to life in Virginia City, the doings of the various mines, rise and fall of mining stocks, etc.. Differing from Fatout's approach, in the author's book about Twain's life in Virginia City, I introduce readers to the men Mark Twain worked with on the *Enterprise* and show how they influenced Twain's writing and career. I also give considerable information about the history and influence of the *Territorial Enterprise* in Nevada and the West.

Ivan Benson's, *Mark Twain in the West*, 1938, was the first book I am aware of that concentrated on Mark Twain's Western years. Well done and useful.

Effie Mono Mack's *Mark Twain in Nevada*, 1947, was the first book to concentrate entirely on Mark Twain's years in Nevada.

Mark Twain in California by Nigey Lennon, 1984, first perked my interest in Twain's life in the West. Good book, easy to read, useful.

What I found very helpful in my own research are the annotated letters of Mark Twain edited by the Mark Twain Project at the University of California at Berkeley and published by the University of California Press. The two I found most useful are *Mark Twain's Letters, Volume 1, 1853-1866* and *Volume 2, 1867-68*. Those fine folks at the Mark Twain Project, in the darkened, still hallways and tiny offices where they work, have done considerable, diligent scholarly research. All of us who write about Twain owe them. (For what it's worth, the Mark Twain Project, due to a recent shortfall in finances, could use your financial support in order to keep their work going. You can contact the project's director, Robert Hirst, by calling the Mark Twain Project at the Bancroft Library, University of California, Berkeley.)

Of the numerous Twain biographies I suggest Albert Bigelow Paine's, *Mark Twain: A Biography*, volumes 1 and 2, and Justin Kaplan's *Mr. Clemens and Mr. Twain*. Paine knew Twain personally and recorded many of the transcriptions Twain dictated for his *Autobiography*. Kaplan's book is astonishingly thorough and gives us a different, and perhaps, more realistic point of view.

A book I found very interesting and useful is *Joseph Hopkins Twichell, Mark Twain's Friend and Pastor*, by Leah A. Strong, which discusses Mark Twain's friendship with Hartford friend Joe Twichell, who seems to have had an undeniable influence on Twain's moral thoughts, family, writing and religious life while Twain lived at Hartford.

Chronology: Mark Twain's Western Years

July 26, 1861: Sam Clemens, at twenty-five, leaves St. Joseph, Missouri by overland stage with his older brother, Orion, recently appointed Secretary of Nevada Territory.
August, 14: Arrives noon at Carson City, Nevada Territory. Rooms with Orion at a boarding house across from the plaza.
Late August: Makes first trip to Lake Tahoe with John Kinney.
Early September: Makes second trip to Lake Tahoe with Tom Nye. Stays three weeks and claims 300 acres of timber. "House" burns down and returns to Carson City.
October: Makes first trip to Aurora, Nevada to inspect the silver mines. Horatio Phillips gives Sam 50 feet in the Black Warrior claim. Returns to Carson City.
October 26: Writes first of several letters published in the Keokuk, Iowa *Gate City*.
November 30: Turn twenty-six.
December 8-16: During this week Sam, Billy Claggett, Jack Simmons and Mr. Tillou leave for Unionville, a silver mining camp 200 miles northeast of Carson City.
December 8-16: After a weary and cold journey, Sam and his friends arrive at Unionville, build a crude shelter and begin prospecting.
Mid-January, 1862: Discouraged with the poor prospects at Unionville, Sam returns to Carson City.
Early April: Takes one of the first stages to Aurora.
April 18: Writes first letter to Orion from Aurora. Begins prospecting and mining with Horatio Phillips and Bob Howland.
May: Begins writing humorous "Josh" letters and sends them to the *Territorial Enterprise* at Virginia City, Nevada, then a booming mining town 15 miles from Carson City.
June 22: Deeply involved with the Annipolitan claim; believes he and Orion will soon be millionaires.
July 30: Receives offer from the *Enterprise* to become a reporter at $25 a week.
August 7: Writes Orion that he has written Barstow of the *Enterprise* and accepted the reporting post.
August 8-15: Makes a walking trip to the White Mountain Mining District, likely Long Valley, site of today's Crowley Lake, near Mammoth Lakes, California east of the Sierra Nevada mountains.
September 9: Writes last letter from Aurora to Billy Claggett.
Mid-September: Arrives in Virginia City having walked 130 miles. Begins work on the *Enterprise* as a local reporter.
October 4: Publishes first hoax, "Petrified Man."
Mid-November through December: In Carson City to report on second Territorial Legislature.
January, 1863: Back in Virginia City as a local reporter.
January 31: Sends a dispatch from Carson City signed "Mark Twain," first time he has used pen name professionally though it appears others were calling him Mark before this dispatch.
Early May: Makes first trip to San Francisco with Clement T. Rice, the Unreliable, reporter for the Virginia City *Union* . Stays one month.
June: Returns to Virginia City.
July 26: White House boarding house on C Street where Twain resides, burns down. Twain loses his clothing and some mining stock.
September 5: Leaves for San Francisco.
Mid-October: Returns to Virginia City. Rooms with Dan De Quille who has recently returned from the East.
October 31: Publishes the infamous "Massacre at Dutch Nick's."
November 1: Admits horrible story was a hoax. Western newspaper editors are outraged. Twain offers to resign from the *Enterprise*.
November 2-December 11: In Carson City to report on Constitutional Convention.
November 30: Turns Twenty-eight.
Early December: Returns to Virginia City for a special presentation when he is given a fake meerschaum pipe by *Enterprise* practical jokers.
About December 7: Returns to Carson City.
December 23-29: Humorist Artemus Ward in Virginia City for several lectures. Twain, Ward and *Enterprise* staff go on one week binge.
January 12-February 20, 1864: In Carson City to report on third Territorial Legislature. Elected "Governor" by Third House.
January 27: Gives first public lecture at Carson City; attracts a large audience at a dollar a head. Donates money to the First Presbyterian Church of Carson City.
February 1: Jennie Clemens, Orion's only daughter, dies of spotted fever.

February 7: "For Sale or to Rent," Twain's first Eastern article published in the New York *Sunday Mercury.*

February 21: "Those Blasted Children," Twain's second Eastern story published in the New York *Sunday Mercury.*

Late February: Returns to Virginia City as local reporter.

February 27: Adah Isaacs Menken, famous actress and hopeful writer, arrives in Virginia City and seeks Twain's friendship.

March 6: First issue of the *Weekly Occidental* , a literary journal, short lived, for which Twain, Tom Fitch and others to collaborate.

April 1: Twain publishes another hoax about rival editor and friend, Tom Fitch, "Another Traitor—Hang Him!"

May 16: Ruel C. Gridley arrives in Virginia City selling the flour sack in efforts to collect money for the Sanitary Fund.

May 17: Twain accuses Carson City ladies of diverting money from the Sanitary Fund to aid the Miscegenation Society.

May 24: Twain denounces Laird of the Virginia *Union* for not accepting his challenge to duel.

May 29: Following a warning from the authorities that he would be arrested for demanding a duel, Twain and Steve Gillis leave Virginia City by stage for San Francisco.

June: Moves into Occidental Hotel in San Francisco.

June 6: Begins reporting for San Francisco *Call.*

June-October 11: Writes for the San Francisco *Morning Call,* denied a by-line and unable to contribute creative articles. Contributes articles to the *Golden Era* and the *Californian* literary journals. Supplies the *Enterprise* with at least one dispatch.

July: Mark and Steve Gillis move into new lodgings, address unknown. Begins submitting articles for the *Californian.*

September 17: Writes Dan De Quille and asks him to buy his Virginia City furniture. Looking for ways to earn money. Quits working nights for the *Call.*

September 28: Writes his older brother, Orion, and asks that his "files," be sent to him, in preparation for writing his first book.

Mid-October: Quits reporting for the *Call.* Concentrates on writing articles for the *Californian,* a West Coast literary journal, for which he is paid $12 each.

Late November: Steve Gillis nearly kills a man in barroom brawl. Mark Twain posts Gillis' bond.

Early December: Mark Twain leaves for Jim Gillis's cabin on Jackass Hill near Sonora. Stays on Jackass Hill through Christmas. Much time is spent telling each other anecdotes and humorous stories.

New Year's, 1865: Spent at Vallecito, Calaveras County, not far from Jackass Hill.

January 3rd: Returns to Jackass Hill with Jim Gillis by way of Angel's Camp and Robinson's Ferry across the Stanislaus River.

January 22nd: At Angel's Camp

January 25th: Twain nearly kills himself at Angel's Camp by falling into a canyon at night. About this time meets Ben Coon at Angel's Hotel, who tells Twain the story of the Jumping Frog.

January 30th: Stays at Angel's Hotel.

February 6: Rain ends. Days are warm and sunny. Begins prospecting around Angel's Camp with Jim Gillis and Dick Stoker.

February 20th: Leaves Angel's Camp for Jackass Hill with Jim Gillis and Dick Stoker in a snow storm.

February 21st: On Jackass Hill again.

February 23rd: Leaves Jackass Hill by horse for Copperopolis.

February 25th: Leaves Copperopolis by stage for San Francisco via Stockton.

February 26th: Home again at the Occidental Hotel in San Francisco. Receives letter from Artemus Ward requesting a story for his upcoming book.

October: Submits "Jim Smiley and His Jumping Frog," for Ward's book. Story arrives in New York too late for publication.

November 18, 1865: "Jim Smiley and His Jumping Frog," sent by Ward's publisher to the editor of New York *Saturday Press,* is published. Story becomes immensely popular and is re-printed by newspapers throughout America and Europe. "Jumping Frog," earns Twain his first national notoriety.

March 7, 1866: Sails to the Sandwich Islands as a correspondent for the Sacramento *Union.*

June 25: Writes dispatch about the burning of the clipper ship, *Hornet,* and its survivors. *Hornet* article helps cement Twain's West Coast career.

October 2: Gives his second humorous lecture on the Sandwich Islands at Maguire's Academy of Music, San Francisco.

October 11: Lectures at Metropolitan Theater, Sacramento.

October 15: Lectures at Marysville Theater, Marysville.

October 23: Lectures at Hamilton Hall, Grass Valley.

October 24: Lectures at Odd Fellows Hall or Log School House at Red Dog.

October 25: Lectures at You Bet.

October 31: Lectures at Piper's Opera House, Virginia City, Nevada.

November 3: Lectures at Carson City Theater, Carson City.

November 7: Lectures at Dayton.

November 9: Lectures at Silver City.

November 10: Lectures at Gold Hill. Robbed by friends on the "Divide."

November 16: Lectures at Platt's Hall, San Francisco.

November 21: Lectures at San Jose.

November 26: Lectures at Petaluma.

November 27: Lectures in Oakland at the College of California.

December 10: Lectures in San Francisco at Congress Hall.

December 15: Leaves California for New York by ship from San Francisco.

June 8, 1867: Sails from New York aboard the *Quaker City* for the Holy Land as a correspondent for the San Francisco *Alta California*.

November 19: Returns to New York. Moves to Washington, D.C. where he begins writing *The Innocents Abroad*, based on letters written for the *Alta California*.

March, 1868: Returns to California in order to secure rights to *Quaker City* letters.

April-June: Continues writing first draft of *The Innocents Abroad* in San Francisco.

April 14: Lectures in San Francisco.

April 15: Lectures again in San Francisco due to demand.

April 18: Lectures at Marysville.

April 20: Lectures at Nevada City.

April 21: Lectures at Grass Valley.

April 27 and 28: Lectures at Piper's Opera House in Virginia City.

April 29 and 30: Lectures at Carson City.

May 1 or about: Returns to Virginia City to visit with Joe Goodman and friends.

May 4: Leaves Carson City for Sacramento.

May 4: Spends the night at Sacramento.

May 5: Back in San Francisco. Rooms at the oppulent Lick House.

May 16: Gives dinner party at the Lick House with burlesque menu, "Lick House State Banquet."

June 17: Rooming at the Occidental Hotel in San Francisco and writing final draft of *The Innocents Abroad*.

July 2: Gives last lecture in San Francisco, Clemens calling it a "farewell benefit of the future widows and orphans of Mark Twain."

July 6: Sails from San Francisco aboard the *Montana*.

July 29: Arrives in New York City.

Mid-1869: *The Innocents Abroad* is published by the American Publishing Company at Hartford.

February 2, 1870: At thirty-four, marries Olivia Langdon.

June 5, 1904: Olivia Langdon Clemens dies.

April 21, 1910: At the age of seventy-four, Mark Twain dies and is buried at Elmira, New York beside Olivia and his daughters, Susy and Jean.

List and dates of publication of Mark Twain's Important Works

Mid-1869: *The Innocents Abroad* published, becomes an immediate success.

February 1872: *Roughing It* published.

December 1873: *The Guilded Age* .

July 21, 1875: *Sketches, New and Old*.

December 1876: *The Adventures of Tom Sawyer*.

March 1880: *A Tramp Abroad*.

January 1882: *The Prince and the Pauper*.

May 1883: *Life on the Mississippi*.

January 1885: *Adventures of Huckleberry Finn*.

December 1889: *A Connecticut Yankee in King Arthur's Court*.

May 1896: *Personal Recollections of Joan of Arc*.

June 1900: *The Man That Corrupted Hadleyburg and Other Stories*.

April 1904: *Extracts from Adam's Diary*.

Selected Bibliography

The following is a partial bibliography students and scholars may find useful.

Unpublished Sources:

The Mark Twain Papers, Mark Twain Project, University of California, Berkeley
William Wright Correspondence, Bancroft Library, University of California, Berkeley.

Newspapers:
Territorial Enterprise
Gold Hill *News*
Virginia *Daily Union*
Virginia *Evening Bulletin*
Virginia *Chronicle*
San Francisco *Call*
San Francisco *Bulletin*
The Californian
The Golden Era
OLD PIUTE
Alta California
Sacramento Union
California Illustrated Magazine

Books and articles:
Barnes, George E. "Mark Twain. As He Was Known During His Stay on the Pacific Slope," San Francisco *Morning Call*, April 17, 1887, page 1.
Benson, Ivan: *Mark Twain's Western Years*, Russell & Russell, 1938.
Branch, Edgar Marquess: *The Literary Apprenticeship of Mark Twain*, University of Illinois Press, 1958; *Clemens of the "Call," Mark Twain in San Francisco*, University of California Press, 1969.
Browne, J. Ross: "A Peep At Washoe," Harper's Monthly XXII, January, 1861.
Browne, Lena F.: *J. Ross Browne: His Letters, Journals and Writing*, University of Mexico Press, 1969.
Clemens, Clara: *My Father Mark Twain*, Harper & Bros., 1931.
Clemens, Susy: *Papa An Intimate Biography of Mark Twain*, edited and an introduction by Charles Neider, Doubleday & Company, Inc., Garden City, New York, 1985.
De Quille, Dan: *The Big Bonanza*, Alfred Knopf, 1947; "Reporting With Mark Twain,"*California Illustrated Magazine, Vol. IV*, 1893; "Artemus Ward In Nevada," *California Illustrated Magazine*, August, 1893.
DeVoto, Bernard: *Mark Twain's America*, Houghton Mifflin Company, 1932
Doten, Alfred: *The Journals of Alfred Doten*, edited by Walter Van Tilburg Clark, University of Nevada Press, 1973; "Early Journalism in Nevada, "The Nevada Magazine, Vol. I, No. 3, 1899.
Fatout, Paul: *Mark Twain in Virginia City*, Indiana University Press, 1964
Frady, Steven R.: *Red Shirts and Leather Helmets*, University of Nevada Press, 1984
Gillis, William: *Memories of Mark Twain and Steve Gillis*, The Banner, 1924
Howells, W.D.: *My Mark Twain*, Harper & Bros., 1911.

Goodwin, Charles C.: *As I Remember Them*, Salt Lake Commercial Club, 1913.

Kaplan, Justin: *Mr. Clemens and Mark Twain*, Simon and Schuster, New York, 1966.

Kelly, J. Wells: *First Directory of Nevada Territory*, San Francisco, 1862; *Second Directory of Nevada Territory*, 1863

Lauber, John: *The Making of Mark Twain*, American Heritage, 1978.

Lennon, Nigey: *Mark Twain in California*, Chronicle Books, 1982.

Lewis, Oscar: *Silver Kings*, Alfred Knopf, 1947.

Long, E. Hudson: *Mark Twain Handbook*, Hendricks House, 1957.

Mack, Effie Mona: *Mark Twain in Nevada*, Charles Scribner's Sons, 1947

Moody, Eric: *Western Carpetbagger*, University of Nevada Press, 1978.

Paine, Albert Bigelow: *Mark Twain: A Biography*, Harper & Bros., 1912. Rogers, Franklin: *The Pattern For Mark Twain's Roughing It*, University of California Press, 1961; Smith, Henry Nash and Anderson,

Frederick: *Mark Twain Of The Enterprise*, University of California Press, 1957.

Stewart, William M.: *Reminiscences*, Neale Publishing Co., 1908.

Strong, Leah A., *Joseph Hopkins Twichell, Mark Twain's Friend and Pastor*

Twain, Mark: *The Autobiography of Mark Twain*, edited by Charles Neider, Harper and Row, 1959; "My Bloody Massacre;" "Curing A Cold;" "My Late Senatorial Secretaryship;" *Roughing It*; *Sketches New and Old*; *The Innocents Abroad*; *Huckleberry Finn; Life on the Mississippi*; *Mark Twain's Letters*, volumes 1 and 2, University of California Press; *Mark Twain's Letters, Vol. 1*, Harper & Bros., 1917. *Mark Twain's Notebook*, Harper & Bros., 1935. *Letters from the Sandwich Islands*, Stanford University Press, 1938; *Mark Twain Speaks for Himself*, edited by Paul Fatout, Purdue University Press, 1978; *Mark Twain Speaking*, edited by Paul Fatout, University of Iowa Press, 1976; *Following the Equator*.

Williams, George J., III: *Mark Twain: His Adventures at Aurora and Mono Lake,* 1987; *Mark Twain: His Life in Virginia City, Nevada,* 1986; *Mark Twain: Jackass Hill and the Jumping Frog,* 1989; Tree By The River Publishing.

Weisenberger, Francis Phelps: *Idol of the West*, Syracuse University Press, 1965.

Index

List of Illustrations

*Order these great books by mail today
Autographed and inscribed by George Williams III.*
Or call **1-800-487-6610** to order with Visa or MasterCard or to request a Free brochure.

PROSTITUTION IN THE NEW WEST
NEW! In the Last of the Wild West. The true story of the author's attempt to expose the murders of prostitutes and corruption in Virginia City, Storey County, Nevada, home of the largest legal brothel in the United States. 264 pages. AUTOGRAPHED. $12.95 quality paperback; $24.95 hard cover.

PROSTITUTION IN THE OLD WEST
ROSA MAY: THE SEARCH FOR A MINING CAMP LEGEND Virginia city, Carson City and Bodie, California were towns Rosa May worked as a prostitute and madam 1873-1912. Read her remarkable true story based on 3 1/2 years of research. Praised by the *Los Angeles Times* and *Las Vegas Review Journal*. Includes 30 rare photos, 26 personal letters. 240 pages. AUTOGRAPHED. $10.95 quality paperback; hard cover, $21.95. Soon to be a television movie.

THE REDLIGHT LADIES OF VIRGINIA CITY, NEVADA Virginia City was the richest mining camp in the American West. The silver from its mines built San Francisco and helped the Union win the Civil War. From 1860-95, Virginia City had three of the largest redlight districts in America. Here women from around the world worked the world's oldest profession. Author Williams tells the stories of the strange lives of the redlight girls, their legends and violent deaths. Based on newspaper accounts, county records and U.S. Census information. Perhaps the best and most informative book on prostitution in the old West. Plenty of historic photos, illustrations, map and letters. 48 pages. AUTOGRAPHED. $5.95 quality paperback; hard cover, $14.95.

HOT SPRINGS
2nd revised edition HOT SPRINGS OF THE EASTERN SIERRA Here are more than 40 natural hot spring pools author George Williams III has located from the Owens Valley, through the Eastern Sierra recreation corridor to Gerlach, Nevada. George has tracked down every hot spring worth "soaking" in. Included are many secret springs only known to locals. George gives easy to follow road directions, and his "2 cents" about each spring are informative and entertaining. Maps by the author help you find these secret springs easily. 80 pages. AUTOGRAPHED. $9.95 quality paperback; hard cover, $12.95.

GHOST TOWNS
THE GUIDE TO BODIE AND EASTERN SIERRA HISTORIC SITES True story of the rise and fall of Bodie, California's most famous mining camp, today a ghost town, National Historic Site and California State Park. Known as the toughest gold mining town in the West where millions were made in a few years, murders were a daily occurrence. Has a beautiful full color cover with 100 photos on an 8 1/2 X 11 format. 88 pages. AUTOGRAPHED. $10.95 quality paperback; hard cover, $21.95.

OUTLAWS
THE MURDERS AT CONVICT LAKE True story of the infamous 1871 Nevada State Penitentiary break in which 29 outlaws escaped and fled more than 250 miles into Mono and Inyo counties, California. They vowed to kill anyone who got in their way. In a terrible shootout at Monte Diablo, today known as Convict Lake just south of Mammoth Lakes ski resort, the convicts killed two men. They fled to nearby Bishop where they were captured and hanged. Includes 18 rare photographs and pen and ink drawings by Dave Comstock. 32 pages. AUTOGRAPHED. $4.95 quality paperback; hard cover, $14.95.

MARK TWAIN IN THE WEST SERIES

MARK TWAIN: HIS ADVENTURES AT AURORA AND MONO LAKE When Sam Clemens arrived in Nevada in 1861, he wanted to get rich quick. He tried silver mining at Aurora, Nevada near Mono Lake not far from Yosemite National Park. Clemens didn't strike it rich but his hard luck mining days led to his literary career. 32 rare photos, mining deeds and maps to places where Clemens lived, wrote and camped. 100 pages. AUTOGRAPHED. $6.95 quality paperback; hard cover, $16.95.

NEW! MARK TWAIN: HIS LIFE IN VIRGINIA CITY, NEVADA While reporting for the *Territorial Enterprise* in Virginia City, 1862-64, Sam Clemens adopted his well known pen name, Mark Twain. Here is the lively account of Mark Twain's early writing days in the most exciting town in the West. Over 60 rare photos and maps to places Twain lived and wrote. 208 pages. AUTOGRAPHED. $10.95 paperback; hard cover, $26.95.

Mark Twain: Jackass Hill and the Jumping Frog by George Williams III. The true story of Twain's discovery of "The Celebrated Jumping Frog of Calaveras County," the publication of which launched his international career. After getting run out of Virginia City, Twain settled in San Francisco in May, 1864. He went to work as a common reporter for the San Francisco *Call*. After five frustrating months, Twain quit the *Call* and began hanging around with Bret Harte, then editor of the popular *Golden Era*, a West Coast magazine. When Twain posted bail for a friend and the friend skipped town, Twain followed and headed for Jackass Hill in the foothills of the Sierra Nevada near Sonora. There Twain lived with his prospector friend Jim Gillis in a one room log cabin on Jackass Hill. After a discouraging prospecting trip, in a saloon at Angel's Camp, Twain was told the Jumping Frog story by a bartender. Twain's version, published eleven months later, became an international hit. "The Celebrated Jumping Frog of Calaveras County," is included in this book.
116 pages, index, bibliography, 35 historic photographs, guide maps for travelers. AUTOGRAPHED. Quality paper $6.95; hard cover $14.95

On the Road with Mark Twain in California and Nevada Here is a handy, easy to read guide to Mark Twain's haunts in California and Nevada 1861-68. Has road directions to historic sites, guide maps and lots of photographs of Twain, the historic sites and Twain's friends. Gives brief run-downs of each place and tells what Twain was doing while there. A must-have book for any Twain fan who would like to follow his trail in the far West. 136 pages, many photos, road maps, index. $14.95 quality paper; $29.95 hard cover.

And on today's Music Business...

2nd revised edition 1994/ The Songwriter's Demo Manual and Success Guide teaches the songwriter and aspiring group how to make a professional "demo" tape at home or in the recording studio. The quality of a demo tape greatly determines whether or not a song is published or a group lands a recording contract. George Williams, a published songwriter, recording studio owner and producer, covers the complete demo process. choosing the songs, rehearsing, arranging, finding an inexpensive studio, how to get free recording time and many more money saving tips. Once the demo is recorded, it must be placed into the hands of the right people. Williams explains how the music business operates, who the important people are, how to make contact with them and how to sell your songs by mail and in person. 200 pages, many photos and illustrations with a comprehensive Appendix listing helpful publications, contacts, songwriter associations, books, etc. $14.95 quality soft cover; $29.95 library hard cover. AUTOGRAPHED BY THE AUTHOR.
"A valuable, well organized handbook and a cogent look at a tough show-business field... just may be the most helpful guide of its kind...could provide the novice with the ticket for success." **Booklist**

See next page for Order Form...

Order Form

To order books **Toll Free** with *VISA* or MasterCard call **1-800-487-6610**, 9AM to 5PM West Coast time Monday through Friday. **Phone orders are shipped the same day received. Call for a Free brochure.**

Name _____

Address_____City_____

State_____Zip_____

Yes, George send me the following books, autographed and inscribed:

____Copy(ies) In the Last of the Wild West, 12.95 pap.; 24.95 hard cover
____Copy(ies) Rosa May: The Search For A Mining Camp Legend, 10.95 pap.; 21.95 hard
____Copy(ies) The Redlight Ladies of Virginia City, 5.95 pap.; 14.95 hard cover
____Copy(ies) Hot Springs of the Eastern Sierra, 9.95 pap.; $14.95 hard cover
____Copy(ies) The Guide to Bodie, 10.95 pap.; 21.95 hard cover
____Copy(ies) The Murders at Convict Lake, 4.95 pap.; 14.95 hard cover
____Copy(ies) Mark Twain: His Adventures at Aurora, 6.95 pap.; 14.95 hard cover
____Copy(ies) Mark Twain: His Life In Virginia City, Nevada, 10.95 pap.; 26.95 hard
____Copy(ies) Mark Twain: Jackass Hill and the Jumping Frog, $6.95 pap.; 14.95 hard cover
____Copy(ies) On the Road with Mark Twain In California and Nevada, 14.95 pap.; 29.95 hard cover
____COPY(ies) The Songwriter's Demo Manual and Success Guide, 14.95 paper; $29.95 hard cover

Shipping by postal service is 2.25 for the first book, .75 each additional book.
Faster shipping via UPS is 3.00 for the first book. 1.00 each additional book.

Total for books_____
Shipping   _____

Total enclosed in check or money order _____
Mail your order to:

Tree By The River Publishing
PO Box 935-O
Dayton, Nevada 89403

Order Form

To order books **Toll Free** with *VISA* or MasterCard call **1-800-487-6610**, 9AM to 5PM West Coast time Monday through Friday. **Phone orders are shipped the same day received. Call for a Free brochure.**

Name _____

Address_____City_____

State_____Zip_____

Yes, George send me the following books, autographed and inscribed:

___Copy(ies) In the Last of the Wild West, 12.95 pap.; 24.95 hard cover
___Copy(ies) Rosa May: The Search For A Mining Camp Legend, 10.95 pap.; 21.95 hard
___Copy(ies) The Redlight Ladies of Virginia City, 5.95 pap.; 14.95 hard cover
___Copy(ies) Hot Springs of the Eastern Sierra, 9.95 pap.; $14.95 hard cover
___Copy(ies) The Guide to Bodie, 10.95 pap.; 21.95 hard cover
___Copy(ies) The Murders at Convict Lake, 4.95 pap.; 14.95 hard cover
___Copy(ies) Mark Twain: His Adventures at Aurora, 6.95 pap.; 14.95 hard cover
___Copy(ies) Mark Twain: His Life In Virginia City, Nevada, 10.95 pap.; 26.95 hard
___Copy(ies) Mark Twain: Jackass Hill and the Jumping Frog, $6.95 pap.; 14.95 hard cover
___Copy(ies) On the Road with Mark Twain In California and Nevada, 14.95 pap.; 29.95 hard cover
___COPY(ies) The Songwriter's Demo Manual and Success Guide, 14.95 paper; $29.95 hard cover

Shipping by postal service is 2.25 for the first book, .75 each additional book.
Faster shipping via UPS is 3.00 for the first book. 1.00 each additional book.

Total for books_____
Shipping   _____

Total enclosed in check or money order _____
Mail your order to:

Tree By The River Publishing
PO Box 935-O
Dayton, Nevada 89403